blue
SCARLET

blue SCARLET

GARY T. BRIDEAU

Blue Scarlet

Published in the United States of America

ISBN: 978-1-64460-063-4 (*sc*)
978-1-64460-062-7 (*e*)

Library of Congress Control Number: 2018964558

Stonewall Press books may be ordered through booksellers or by contacting:

Stonewall Press
4800 Hampden Lane, Suite 200
Bethesda, MD 20814 USA
www.stonewallpress.com
1-888-334-0980
orders@stonewallpress.com

Science Fiction
18.11.22

About the Galaxy Sentinel series

Thor, or Thor Manning Stromburg, is the Galaxy Sentinel, who is six feet tall, with deep brown hair and rugged features. He oversees the Institute complex that sits on top of a mountain, jungle-dominated planetoid.

The Institute building is a five-story red brick building that houses the galaxy's most feared and dangerous criminals, who are guarded by a highly-trained staff of two hundred and fifty men and women.

Thor does not work above the law, he works with the law tracking down hardened criminals and locking up, out of society's way for good.

The law of the Planetary Alliance says, that if felon is caught committing a crime. There is no trial to find out if he is guilty, his actions are a testamentary against him therefore he is without excuse, but a hearing is held to decide the criminal sentence. No lawyer, no long drawn out trial. The man was caught, in the middle of committing a crime.

However, if there is a shadow of a doubt whether he is or not guilty. There is a trial to decide his fate.

Thor's wife, Cherry Ruth Blossom, a six feet tall shapely woman with brown hair, stands by his side no matter what. She was born on Planet Haskell Prime, which is slightly smaller, then that of Earth. Cherry's younger sister's name was, Jasmine disappeared and was presumed dead, at the age of sixteen. But she was found later, on Earth.

Cherry's father died in a fiery crash, while serving on an ore spaceship when, she was five years old. From that time on, Cherry and her mother lived on what they could afford, which was not much. As the years went by Cherry received Christ at the age of eighteen and developed an attitude, that she had to work extra hard, for the simple things in life. At the age of twenty, misfortune hung over Cherry's head like a cloud when she struck out on her own and went from one dead-end job to the next.

At the age of thirty, Cherry finally landed an excellent job and a wonderful place to live. When tough times struck, causing her to lose her job and her home all in the same day. Distressed about her life she sat under a Cherry tree in a park weeping not knowing to do next. That's when Thor found her, and they became the first, husband and wife retrieval team in the galaxy.

The Galaxy series also consists of Leprechauns, Sprites, Will-o-the-wisps, and various types of aliens. The Institute is a vast complex consisting, an Arboretum, a beach at the foot of the mountain, a large housing complex, with a cafe, a large store, and a Three-Dimensional Particle Acceleration System on the fifth floor of the Institute that is far better than any hologram, and an underground tramway.

Story line

Someone is wants to take down Thor, the Galaxy Sentinel by using innocent lives. So, Thor has to find a way to stop the mysterious red mist that quickly devours quickly flesh that appears after an explosion in an area crowded with people. Before hundreds of people die.

Contents

About the Galaxy Sentinel series 5
Story line 7

Chapter 1 Entrapment 11
Chapter 2 The Downfall of The She Devils 17
Chapter 3 Close to Home 26
Chapter 4 Back to Mr. Tatsuya 34
Chapter 5 Fritz 42
Chapter 6 Welcome to The Planet, Montros 50
Chapter 7 The Agatharchides Valley 58
Chapter 8 The Will-o'-the-wisp On the Attack 65
Chapter 9 The Tomb 72
Chapter 10 The Woman in The Water 79
Chapter 11 The Dead Forest 86
Chapter 12 Undercover 94
Chapter 13 Moonbeam on The Loose 103
Chapter 14 More Clues 111
Chapter 15 Woody's Back 119
Chapter 16 The Dead Forest Melee 127
Chapter 17 The Attack on Arrgua 135
Chapter 18 Too Close to Home 144
Chapter 19 The hunt 153
Chapter 20 Mandroid Constance 160
Chapter 21 The Mad World 168
Chapter 22 Agar's Last Stand 176

Epilogue 179

CHAPTER 1

Entrapment

A tall voluptuous woman in her mid-thirties, with long wavy hair, clad in a tight black dress, with a plunging neck line. Parked her red, sports hover car in the travel complex on the planet, Dicapl and watched the people coming and going. She spotted a young man in a gray business suit, getting out of his car, walked up to him, and asked, "Been traveling long?"

The young traveler smiled and replied, "You don't know the half of it, ma'am. All I want to do is to find a motel, take a shower and crash for a week."

"I know exactly, what you mean. Those long car trips can take a lot out of you. Oh, I'm Stella Swaddling. Let me buy you, a cup of coffee."

"Thanks, but I must be going."

Stella smiled and said in a soft voice, "Why don't you come home with me. You can take a nice hot shower, enjoy my dessert and sleep in a soft warm bed."

The man pondered Stella's offer for a minute and said, "After you."

Stella parked her car in the driveway to her A-framed house and went inside with the traveler and said, "I didn't get your name."

"It's Walter Zimp."

"Help yourself to a cold drink, while I go and change into something less binding." Stella approached Walter five minutes later, wearing a thin, red, lingerie and asked, "You want me to fix you something to eat?"

Walter studied at Stella's shapely figure underneath her red, flimsy intimate apparel and muttered, "Yeah sure."

"Why don't you get out of those clothes you've had on, for who knows how long and take a shower while I fix you something to eat. There is a bathrobe on the bathroom door, you can put on after."

After his shower, Walter put on the long, green silk robe, sat at the counter, and enjoyed a hearty meal. When he stood up, Stella walked up to him and pressed her body against his saying, "What do you say we have the dessert, now."

In bed, Walter cuddled next to Stella and she whispered, "It's time for you to do something for me." and swiftly slapped a chemical soaked gauze over Walter's mouth, temporarily paralyzing him. She then rolled him on his back and gently rubbed a white numbing cream on his abdomen. With a laser scalpel in her hand, she kissed Walter's lips, saying, "I am going to open you up, and put this grapefruit size blue sphere in your stomach that will explode when the acid in your stomach dissolves the outer casing. No, big deal. You can look in the mirror and see what I am doing."

Walter's eyes widened in terror, as he watched Stella perform the operation. When she had sealed the wound with a healing generator, she lay on top of Walter, kissed him, and placed a disk to his forehead and instructed, "Walter Zimp. You will not remember the operation, just the pleasurable time, you had with me. Tomorrow after the morning meal, I will drive you back to the travel center; you will get in your car and drive to the Metro-plex Mall. There, you will sit, in the busy section and wait until noon." Stella took off the disk and snuggled up to Walter, until morning.

In the morning, Stella rubbed Walter's shoulder's and asked, "Ready for round two?"

No, I have to be at the Metro-plex Mall before noon. Could you take me there?"

Clad in skimpy attire, Stella fussed over Walter making sure, she was the only thing on his mind when she sent him on his way.

At noon, a tremendous explosion rocked the mall and a blue gas bellowed up from Walter's remains, dissolving all living tissue that it came in contact with.

On the other side of town, Peggy, a medium built woman with short black hair, clad in a burgundy dress, sat at the counter in a White Forest Cafe, in Posa City, on the planet Avalon Prime. She handed the crystal flash drive to Thor, a six-foot-tall man with deep brown hair and a rugged looking and stated, "All the information you need on the Blue Scarlet project is on here."

Thor took the crystal and stated, "I'll make sure, you are protected from the scientist.

Just then, Peggy's computer watch rang, she answered, saying, "Good day to you, Sir."

A blurred image of a woman's head appeared over her computer watch and, a garbled voice asked, "Did you think you could betray me and get away with it? Did you? Oh, I have a little something for you."

Peggy grew nervous, touched Thor's arm saying, "I'll contact you later this evening." She stood and turned to go when a sharp pain gripped her stomach, she glanced down at the blood oozing from a wound looked at Thor and fell to the floor dead. Shot with a poison dart.

Stella stuck her energy pistol in Thor's back and demanded, "I'll take that crystal storage thank you."

"You think I am going to give this to you,"

"Hand, it over, or die, Sentinel."

Thor eyed her high-pressure air gun, grabbed that with his left hand, to deliver a deadly blow with his right. But, he was stunned from an energy blast that sent him to the floor.

Ten minutes later, Thor knelt, touched Peggy's side, and vowed to take down her killer.

The police rushed in and inquired, "What happened here, Sentinel?"

"A woman killed Peggy. I tried to vaporize her, but, she stunned me instead."

"I thought the Galaxy Sentinel never killed anyone."

"Too many thugs have been getting away with murder here of lately and it's time for a change."

"I'll agree with you, on that. Oh, the Blue Scarlet struck again, this time at the Metro-plex Mall. Some poor guy by the name of Walter Zimp was splattered all over the place when the bomb in him exploded."

"How bad is it?"

"The same, skeletal remains of men, women and children dripping with a blue caustic chemical that we can't figure out."

"What about this Walter Zimp? Do you know who he was?"

"He was a business man with a wife, two children and no criminal record. Go figure."

Thor held up the crystal flash drive and stated, "Peggy gave me this before she was killed. What the woman took from me was a copy of Cherry's cookie recipes."

"Smart thinking, Sir."

"It's time, this Blue Scarlet character, met the Galaxy Sentinel and you know what's gonna happen."

"Yeah, the one who's sending out the Blue Scarlet will have, to kiss their butt good-bye. Don't worry about it. I've got you covered."

"Oh, I want what's left of Walter and the other remains sent to the Institute to be examined. See ya later; I have to meet my wife, at The God Sent Diner."

Outside, Thor touched his computer watch and stated, "Sprite Dr., Chrissy, there was another Blue Scarlet attack and I am having all the remains sent to you. Have the lab do a complete toxicology and a DNA scan, on all of them. Thor, out."

At the 'God Sent Diner,' Thor kissed his wife, and sat in a booth with her and ordered a thick juicy, stake medium rear, with onion gravy, mashed potatoes, and corn. While Cherry ordered the Almond Crushed Tilapia with rice and string beans. Cherry asked, as she took a bite of her fish. "Did you find out what Peggy wanted?"

"Oh yeah. She gave me the information on Blue Scarlet. However, she was murdered by Stella who demanded that I give her the disk." Thor cringed and said, "Sorry Hon. Your cookie recipes fell into the wrong hands, instead of your friend."

Cherry snickered and said, "In my haste this morning, I accidentally gave you the wrong flash drive. What I gave you was a blank crystal storage flash-drive."

Thea, a woman in her late 50s walked up to them and inquired, "What would you like for dessert? Pie, Ice cream, chocolate velvet cake, or a big slice of rich creamy strawberry delight?"

Cherry muttered, "Well there goes my diet. 2 sliced of strawberry delight with lots of whip cream. If I am going to blow it, I might as well do it big time."

Thor remark, "Kinda slow, today."

"Tuesdays are always slow."

Stella marched in the diner, sat next to Cherry, and stated through clinched teeth, "Give me the right flash drive, or I kill your wife."

"Oh, hi Stella. Would you like whip cream with your dessert?"

"Give it to me, now!"

Thor quickly threw his ice water in Stella's face, and grabbed the energy pistol out of her hand; Stella stared at Thor, as her body stiffened, went into convulsions, and fell face first on the table with a smoke rising from her ears.

Thor stared at her and stated, "How about that, she is an android." He tapped his computer watch and said, "Teeny, I need your expertise at 'The God Sent Diner, right away. I have a dead android on my hands."

"A what?" questioned Teeny in shock.

"A fried female android."

"Are you sure it's deceased?"

"It's hot to the touch and smoke is coming out of her ears, nose and mouth."

"It's toast. I'll be there in a jiffy." Teeny out.

Thea stared at the android, then at the door and asked, "Can you bring it in the other part of the diner, so my customers won't think I am serving nasty food."

"Consider it done."

Thirty-seven minutes later, Teeny a midget, stood next to Cindy, his android who stood six feet tall with blond hair, clad in a paisley dress, glanced at Stella lying on the floor and stated, "Thor I'm afraid its circuitry is fried. How did it happen?"

"She was going to kill Cherry if I didn't give her the flash drive, so I threw water in her face, but, I guess, she was the cat's paw in all this."

Teeny knelt, unbuttoned Stella's blouse, pushed her bellybutton, causing a section, from her breast to her hips to slide upwards. Teeny removed her midsection and studied the android's mechanism and said, "Everything looks good down here, let me check the microprocessor in her head." Teeny stuck a long, thin screwdriver in Stella's left ear, then removed her entire face and exclaimed, "Whoa! It's burnt to a crisp! Let me check her backup memory just, for G and C." Thor helped Teeny roll Stella over on her stomach, removed the back panel from her neck, stuck a crystal memory flash drive in the slot and uploaded 7 and a half Terabytes of information. Looked up at Thor and said, "Give me a week to study this stuff, then I'll get back to you."

Teeny put the android back together, had Thor stand her on her feet and asked, "You wanna carry her, out to my car?"

CHAPTER 2

The Downfall of The She Devils

Back at the institute, Thor entered the infirmary and questioned Dr. Chrissy, a 36 inches' tall sprite with wavy brown hair. "Have you examined the remains I sent you?"

"Yes. So far what I can figured out is the stuff that devolves flesh off their bodies was, Hydrochloric acid with a powerful accelerant which caused them to die a quick but, agonizing death. I'll have all their DNA within the hour."

Thor approached Moonbeam, a 36 inches' tall sprite with yellow hair, in the hallway clad in bright yellow bra and underwear and inquired, "You want to explain to me why you are walking around the halls in your underclothes?"

"It's the new cotton bathing suit, Sir and it meets with all the Institute standards."

Thor carefully studied the sprite's so-called swimwear and said, "You're pushing it Moonbeam." Thor went to walk away, paused, turned around, stared at Moonbeam, and questioned, "By any chance did 4 sprites by the name of, Mimi, Darlene, Constance, and Susanna tell you this?"

"Why yes. How did you know? I was in the Arboretum when I met them by the circular garden. Constance gave me this expensive bathing suit out of the kindness of her heart."

Thor smiled, stated softly, "They pulled a fast one on you."

Moonbeam's face turned red from embarrassment and stated, "You mean I've been walking around in public in my unmentionables?"

"I'm afraid so."

Moonbeam clenched her fist and screamed, "I'm gonna kill them! So, help me I am!"

Thor entered his office with Moonbeam and asked his secretary Lacy, a petite young woman, with light brown wavy hair said, "You're looking fine today. Any calls while I was out?"

"Miss Franks is waiting for you in your inner office."

"Lacy, see what you can do to dig up some clothes for Moonbeam."

"Did Constance and her 3 devilish cohorts strike again?"

"You guessed it."

Lacy stared at Moonbeam trying to keep a straight face.

Moonbeam's eyes narrowed and growled, "Don't even think of it Lacy."

"Too late. Nice yellow undies."

"I still say it's a cotton bathing suit."

"Suit yourself. Oh, ah your bathing suit has a hole in it."

"Where?"

"On your butt."

Moonbeam let go a squeal, placed her hands behind and said, "On second thought, I'll take whatever clothes you have."

"All I have is this bumblebee costume."

Thor entered his inner office, saw Miss Franks and inquired, "How is everything going with King Mex?"

"Good, but I would 1 like your permission to live here and commute there everyday."

"You are the ambassador and that means you live there. You move back here, and I will promptly dismiss you."

"But Sir I'm cramped in those small sprites houses."

"Do I need to remind you because of your poor conduct you were to be the Ambassador, to the Sprites? That's what the agreement was. Or have you forgotten?"

Miss Franks hung her head and said, "I remember, Sir."

"Why don't you have the King build you a home that you can live in? Instead of trying to live in that cramped tiny house?"

Miss Franks smiled and said, "Thanks Sir. I never thought of that. I'll return immediately to get my new house built."

Lacy announced over the intercom, "Miss Vilma Puckett is here to see you Sir."

A medium built woman with long black hair dressed in a green lab coat entered and said, "I have something I think you would like to see."

"Lead the way."

Thor entered a large room filled with racks of test tubes, and computers. Miss Puckett brought Thor into a long dark room with a lit stage at one end. She pointed to a sheet of gray sheet metal, picked up an Earth style nine-millimeter pistol. Fires several rounds and then fired blast of energy vaporizing the sheet metal and said, "That type of metal is used for siding on our houses. If we were attacked and the energy shield failed, we would be in big trouble. However, I have come up with a new paint that will protect anything it is applied, observe."

A sheet of metal sprayed with white paint was lowered into position. Miss Puckett fired several rounds at it barely scratching the surface. She then fired a ten second blast from a high-energy rifle at the sheet of metal, leaving it unscathed.

Thor commented, "Impressive. Does the paint come in different collars or just white?"

"Any color you like sir."

"How soon can you have enough of this super paint to begin painting the homes?"

"Next week Sir."

"Great. Go for it."

"Oh, and Sir. I have duplicated the Blue Scarlet acid and I'm working on a way to neutralize it."

"Have you figured out what that stuff doesn't eat through?"

"Yes. My Super Paint."

"Keep working on it Miss Puckett, you'll come up with a solution."

On the way, back to his office, Thor met Moonbeam in the hall tugging on her shorts, grumbling, "Stupid shorts are too small. But, I should be thankful Mary Bell left a pair behind just in case of an emergency."

Thor touched Moonbeam's shoulder and questioned, "Eating too much Pylean donuts?"

Moonbeam squealed and jumped, then turned around and said, "Sir! Where did you come from? I was on my way to the Sprite security office to check in."

"Just be on time tomorrow morning and wear something more than those shorts that are too tight for you."

"But sir? It was not my fault."

"In a way, it was. Because you allowed yourself to be fooled by those four she devils."

Moonbeam hung her head and said, "You are right Sir."

Thor knelt, gave the troubled sprite a hug saying, "Just keep your wits about you when you are around, Constance, Mimi, Darlene and Susanna and you will do fine."

Moonbeam entered her office, contacted Constance and said, "The Sprite security is having a beach party this evening, you and your friends, Mimi, Darlene, and Susanna are more than welcome to come. Oh, don't forget to stop by my office for free bug repellent."

Moonbeam dumped out the contents of 4 plastic spray bottles that was filled with bug repellent and filled them with her own concoction that would attract every stinging insect in the area. Then gave them to Constance and her 3 friends saying, "You 4 are going to be attractive tonight in your new bathing suits."

That evening, a large number of male and female sprites gathered by the natural waterside on the far end of the beach. There was a smorgasbord of food and drinks for everyone along with plenty of wholesome fun for all.

However, for some strange reason Constance, Mimi, Darlene, and Susanna slapped themselves silly all evening trying to keep away all the little bloodsucking insects. As the crowd was thinning out, Moonbeam approached, Constance, Mimi, Darlene, and Susanna and stated firmly. You 4 will report for duty tomorrow morning. You are now part of the Sprite Security."

"You can't do that to us!" screamed Susanna, "Who's the boss of that chicken outfit now that Mary Bell left?"

"Me. And yes I can, because you 4 have walked around this top-secret installation like it was you own the place long enough. You have 2 choices, be thrown in the slammer for 15 years for trespassing on government property. Or serve in the Sprite Security and get paid next to nothing, free housing, with me as your boss."

"Why the sudden change?" questioned Darlene, "Mary Bell never mentioned anything like that to us."

"When you 4 tricked me into wearing that updated style bathing suit that was in reality underwear, you picked on the wrong person. Now your butts are mine."

Darlene grumbled, "I told you Constance that it was a stupid idea. But no, you three blockheads did it anyways."

"Who got the underwear?" snapped Constance.

Moonbeam barked, "Alright you 4 slackers! I want to see this beach in pristine condition before you leave! Now, move it! Oh, those bathing suits I had you put on, is underwear. Now move it!"

"You can't order me around like that." snapped Susanna.

Moonbeam grabbed Susanna by her top and growled, "I own you for the next 5 years' sister. Now, move that scrawny sit-down of yours!"

Constance got in Moonbeam's face and stated, "Girls, don't touch a thing. I'm going to talk to Thor, then we will see."

Moonbeam escorted the 4 sprites to Thor's cottage and knocked on the door. Cherry answered and asked, "How was the party?"

Constance quickly bellowed, "Moonbeam is telling us that we have to work for the Sprite Security or be thrown in the clink for 15 years for trespassing on a government installation."

Cherry remained silent for a minute then said, "Moonbeam is right. You four have been getting away with way too much. Now you 4 are walking around in your underwear. That is crossing the line."

Moonbeam marched the four sprites back to the picnic area and ordered, "Okay you four good for nothings, All I want to see is a blur! Now, move it!"

"Can we at least get dressed." asked Mimi.

"One more word out of ether one of you and you'll be cleaning this beach in your birthday suits!"

Two hours later, the four sprites stood erect in front of Moonbeam and Constance asked, "Now, can we go home?"

"There is a piece of paper by Susana's right foot that needs to be picked up. Then you will report to Rock's security and he will put you up in some of the guest rooms for the night. Then tomorrow you will be assigned a house."

"But what about our apartments across the lake?" questioned Mimi.

"I will appoint some of the sprites to help you move. Remember tomorrow morning at my office at eight sharp. Now, get lost."

Mimi lingered, stared at Moonbeam sheepishly and said, "Sir. Can I talk to you for a moment?"

"Sure. What's on your mind?"

"I suffer from Lachanophobia."

"I'll see what I can do to keep you away from vegetable gardens. Oh Mimi, could you do me a favor? Keep an eye on Constance for me. I'll add an extra fifty dollars in your pay for your troubles."

Constance clenched her fists and let out a long frustrating scream. When she was finished, Moonbeam questioned, "Feel better?"

After the four sprites left for the Institute, Moonbeam fell on the ground laughing until her sides hurt.

The next morning, Mimi, Darlene and Susanna reported to Moonbeam for duty, Moonbeam, questioned "Where is Constance?"

Mimi answered, "She is home tending to her garden, I think."

Moonbeam contacted Tippy and asked, "Can you and your sister do me a favor? I have a delinquent by the name of Constance that needs to be caught and brought into my office, A-S-A-P."

Twenty minutes later, Thor's two adopted daughters; Tippy who resembled a tall slender six-foot pixie called a Will-o-the-wisp, and

Abbie a young female Will-o-the-wisp with white fuzzy wings, dragged Constance in Moonbeam's office in her short nightgown and said, "Here she is. Do you want us to flog her?"

"No just a little torture will do,"

Constance stood and bellowed, "What is the meaning of this? You will hear from my lawyer for having me kidnapped in my nightclothes!"

Moonbeam glared at the stubborn sprite and stated, "You were instructed to be in my office no later than eight o'clock, it is now ten forty-five. Here is your uniform, put it on. Your duty today is to patrol the metroplex."

"I will not. I have to tend to my garden."

"Okay, if that is the way you want to play. Tippy, Abbie, take off Constance's nightgown and pull down her underwear, so I can insert a tracking ball in her butt cheek."

With Constance's nightwear on the floor, and her underwear down to her feet, Tippy and Abbie forcefully bent Constance over a wooden chair with her hollering in protest, "You can't do this to me!" when she felt the sharp needle touch her butt she thought, "Oh God no, they're going to do it," and screamed, "Alright! I'll do whatever you say, Boss Moonbeam. Just don't put that needle in me!"

"Too late to stop now," Constance screamed, "Please don't, it hurts, it hurts!"

Later, dressed in her uniform, Constance rubbed her posterior saying, "One day Moonbeam you will get yours."

Moonbeam ordered, "You and your friends, Mimi, Darlene, and Susanna are going to go to Mary Bell's home with cake and flowers and apologize to her for all the stupid tricks you pulled on her in the past. Then, you do your rounds."

"Do we have to kiss her feet too?" questioned Darlene.

"Don't get smart with me. Oh, you have the weekends off, so you can go home and rest up. But you have to be back for work on Mondays."

"Where do we stay in the meantime?"

"See Cathy Loganberry after work, she will assign you four, a house."

Tippy smiled as she watched Constance leave and commented, "You did Good Moonbeam. It is great to see the death to those 4 She devils Mimi, Darlene, Susanna and Constance."

"Moonbeam stood up picked up a folder off her desk and said, "Tippy, Abbie I have to give Thor the report. Talk to you later."

Moonbeam entered Thor's office, handed him the report and stated, "We have got to do something about Sprite Jed. He keeps flying over the house on the street that border the jungle when he is not supposed to. I have warned him several times, but he doesn't listen to me. I have even given him time off because of his actions, but he still persists."

"Have you had any complaints?"

"Yes, Cathy, Fara, Miss Puckett, Pixy, just to name a few. All of them are accusing Jed of spying on them. Fare went outside in her undies one afternoon, to get something and glanced up and saw Jed looking at her."

"Is she sure it was Jed and not another Peeping Tom?"

"Okay. This is the way the complaints go. A male sprite is seen flying over the backyards in the evening just before Jed shift ends."

"All the sprite guards wear the same uniform, so how can they say that it is Jed that is spying on them."

"Of course, Jed is denying the accusations."

"He keeps telling me that he is not the reprobate that is doing it."

"This is what you do. Let up on Jay, but have Cathy do a DNA scan the next time he flies over the houses, then we will do a match and catch him that way."

Moonbeam placed a diagram of a tunnel on Thor's desk and said, "Sir. There is a growing problem with too many motorized carts on the beach which makes it almost difficult for the bathers. What I propose is we dig a tramway to the beach. There is a section by the metroplex where we can bore straight down, build the depot, then bore out to the beach. It will make it easier for everyone."

"The tramway should be on a loop with one car on each end. But where do you think tunnel should come up?"

“Right on the jungle’s edge between the waterside and the beach house.” stated Moonbeam.

“The elevator on the beach leading down to the tramway, should resemble a tree.”

“Yes, yes, yes, yes!” shouted Moonbeam with excitement, “Can we do It, Sir?”

“I’ll give you all the information you need to get the project started. Contact Sam for the boring machine.”

Just as Moonbeam gave Thor a hug, Cherry, a six feet tall shapely woman with brown hair, walked in and quipped, “Trying to steal Thor away from me Moonbeam?”

Moonbeam spun around and with a surprised look on her face and said, “Mrs., Thor, A Cherry, it was just a friendly hug. I’m not after your hubby, honest.”

“It’s the quiet ones that you have to watch out for.”

Moonbeam’s wings wilted as her countenance fell and stated, “You are so right. You caught me trying to get friendly with Thor.” She turned around, bent over, and said, “You can kick my sit-down as hard as you like.”

“Alright here goes, but first I need to see what I am kicking.” Cherry walked up to the sprite and made as if she was going to pull her slacks down but dropped two ice-cubes down the back of her undies. Moonbeam, quickly straightened up and hollered, “Wow, that’s cold!” and danced around the office trying to shake the ice out of her pants.

Once she was free from cubes, Moonbeam smiled up at Cherry and said, “Good one. Hi-five.” and left.

Cherry sat on Thor’s desk hiked her dress up to her thighs and asked, “You doing anything this afternoon? There is this spot by Lake Mary Bell where we can be alone for hours without anyone seeing us.”

Lacy paged Thor over the intercom and said, “Sorry for interrupting but, Chrissy want to see you.”

Thor rubbed his wife’s thigh and said, “Duty calls. But, hold that thought for me will ya.”

CHAPTER 3

Close to Home

Thor entered the infirmary and inquired, "What's up Chrissy?"

"The bones of the victims have become brittle and I had to dispose of all the remains because of the caustic vapor rising from them. So, I burned them, put each of their ashes in a pretty container and sent them to the families for burial. Now, I am waiting on Miss Puckett to find out what she came up with."

"Do you have any clues as to who is killing all these people?"

"The scientist, Mr. Tatsuya, has a dark sinister sided to his personality. If you ask me, I think that scientist and the Hummer-Gene that killed Joanna and not just the Hummer-Gene." Chrissy stared at Thor in silence, then stated, "What if it isn't acid we are dealing with but a chemical that breaks down the molecular cohesion in the body the same way the Hummer-Gene's staff, did?"

"Do you think Mr. Tatsuya can adjust his invention to match the energy frequency of the Hummer-Gene's staff?" inquired Thor.

"Can you bring his invention here? Miss Puckett and I will do the rest."

"What do you have in mind Doctor?"

"If Miss Puckett and I can duplicate the Blue Scarlet results by using Mr. Tatsuya's invention, we might have the one who's behind the Blue Scarlet attacks."

"Sam and I will get right on it."

"Don't forget to call the police station for a search warrant."

"Don't need one. I'm the Galaxy Sentinel. If I have probable cause then I can connect Mr. Tatsuya's invention to the attacks, so I can confiscate his invention just like that."

The royal blue macaw named, Horatio flew in, lit on Thor's shoulder and stated, "Pardon for the interruption, Boss. But Cherish is approaching the building with a bomb in her abdomen."

Thor glanced at his watch and said, "It's almost noon. He tapped the intercom and stated, "Doc. meet me outside with your medical bag. We have an emergency. Lacy, erect the energy shield around the building now!"

Thor met Cherish as she was about to enter the building and suggested, "Why don't you rest in the Arboretum before lunch."

"No, I have to be inside."

Thor forcefully escorted Cherish away from the building, As Doc. Chrissy rushed outside, did a medical scan on Cherish and exclaimed, "Oh Lord, No!" Injected her with a sedative and ordered, "Thor bring her into Star Fire Two and have Cherry prep her for sugary."

"Inside the spacecraft, Thor placed Cherish in a bunk removed her slacks and blouse then asked, "Now what?"

"Help me shove this tube down her throat so I can pump a mild acid neutralizing solution in her stomach, get me a bucket of water then leave."

The staff gathered at the front of the Institute, praying. Cherry walked up to her husband, put her arms around his arm and inquired, "What's wrong with my twin sister?"

"She has a Blue Scarlet bomb in her stomach. If the doctor isn't swift enough with her scalpel, that thing in Cherishes stomach will goes off. Which means we're in big trouble."

The staff members stared at the spacecraft as the minutes slowly ticked by, wondering if they were going to die an agonizing death. When Chrissy exited the craft ten minutes later and waved that everything was clear. Cherry rushed up to Chrissy with Thor and she asked, "How is she doing, "Cherish will be on antibiotics for a while because I had to operate without scrubbing up first. But, she will live." Chrissy handed Thor the bucket of water with the blue grapefruit size orb in it and said, "Handle it carefully, it may rupture at the slightest jar."

Thor put the bucket down and stood back, drew his energy pistol, and vaporized it with a single blast of energy. Then touched his computer watch and said, "Lacy, put the Institute on yellow alert and recall all personal." Thor stared at Cathy Loganberry, a five foot, five inches tall young woman with long light brown hair and glasses clad in jeans tending to Horatio. Walked up to her and stated, "Thank you because if it wasn't for Horatio the Institute would be littered with our skeletal remains. Thank you." Thor than announced, "Okay, shows over back to work!"

Minutes later, Thor entered his office and found a tall man dressed in tan pants and white shirt with a crew-cut, sitting behind his desk with his feet up. He grinned at Thor and said, casually, "I forgot about that bird of yours would pick up the Blue Scarlet device. Next time you will not be so lucky.

"There won't be a next time and get out of my chair."

He picked up a picture of Cherry on Thor's desk and said, "You have a beautiful wife. It would be a shame if she was caught in a cloud Blue Scarlet. I've been told that during those few seconds they're being dissolved the pain is excruciating."

"That's it you piece of scum!" screamed Thor. He latched on the man's shoulders and hauled him over the top of his desk then threw him across his office. The man rose to his feet, took a fighting stance, and stated, "I hear that there is a picnic in the park next week. How well can you handle four of Blue Scarlet bombs?"

The gruesome remains of the innocent men and women in the mall flashed through Thor's mind. He clenched his fist and stated, "You heartless sadistic monster." Picked him up and threw him through the solid oak office door. The man staggered to his feet and hollered, "You can't stop the destruction that is about to come upon the Alliance."

Sam rushed in and began to hammer the man's face with his fist. Thor hollered, "It's a trap! Lacy set the Retrieval Computer for deep space!"0.

Thor picked up the man threw him on the pad as Lacy activated the computer, seconds before he exploded."

Thor fell to the floor, leaned back against a wall looked up at Sam and said, "That was too close. Sam sat next to Thor and said, "You up to paying Mr. Tatsuya a visit?"

"In a bit. Right now, I could go for a cup of coffee."

Lace handed Thor and Sam their coffee, placed a plate of donuts between them and said, "Enjoy."

Cherry rushed in saw the mess and asked, "What happened?"

"We were hit with a one two punch. There was a man in my office with a Blue Scarlet orb in him."

"I had that bird that Cathy tinkered together fly around and scan the area for any more bombs."

"You mean the royal blue macaw, Horatio? What I like to know is how they got by the senor net."

"More over guys, I'm gonna join you."

"I'll get you a cup of coffee."

Gideon the 2-foot-tall, Three-Dimensional Particle Acceleration bear, clad in a green and gold kimono walled up to Thor with blood on his katana.

Thor asked, "What's up, Squirt?"

Gideon pointed towards the door and waddled off.

"Okay Squirt, I'm right behind you. Come on Sam, let's go see what Gidester has caught."

Cherry grabbed the last doughnut and rushed off with her mug of coffee in one hand and a doughnut in the other.

Outside, Thor glanced down, saw a young, slender woman on the ground by the Arboretum, being guarded by the security with a gash in her leg and he questioned, "Tammy Lee. What are you doing here and how did you get on this planetoid without proper clearance?"

"Did you forget, I am an Agent for the Alliance and I have a 4-star clearance, or did you forget? Now, call off your goons and get me to your health facility before I bleed to death."

"You never answered my question. "How did you get on this top-secret planetoid?"

"I told you, I used my 4-star security clearance, punched in this location, entered my clearance access code, and came here so you can take me to Earth. Now, get me some medical help before I bleed to death!"

"You are lucky that Gideon didn't dice you up. The next time you go through popper channels and use the Retrieval Computer. Security, bring her to Sprite Doctor Chrissy."

"No, wait! I want the doctor to come to me."

Thor touched his computer watch and said, "Chrissy, there is a medical emergency by the Arboretum."

The Doc. flew out the door, landed by Tammy Lee, stared at her gash, and asked, "You called me out here for a scratch?"

Tammy glared at the doctor and grumbled, "You have got to be kidding me? That's your doctor? She barely comes up to my knees."

Doc. Chrissy opened her green medical bag, took out her 6-inch-long medical needle and ordered, Cherry, pull Tammy's slacks and underwear down, feet so I can give her a shot in the rump."

Tammy Shouted, "Whoa! Get that harpoon away from me!"

"Then, get your fanny up off the ground and walk in the infirmary so I can treat you. If not, you can stay here and bleed."

"Miss Chrissy Baker Windstrum!" shouted Tammy Lee, "You mean you are going to let me lie here and bleed to death?"

"Don't look now, but, it has already stopped bleeding."

Cherry put Tammy in a head lock, Chrissy yanked down Tammy's slacks and underwear and jabbed her butt with the needle.

Tammy screamed, "Ouch that hurts! Get that harpoon out of my butt right this minute!"

Cherry let go of Tammy, she pulled her slacks up and grumbled, "How dare you expose me to all the man walking by."

"What men? It's just Thor and he had his back turned."

Tammy glared at Cherry and stormed off.

Thor asked, "Chrissy, you know her?"

"I have had the pleasure of treating her several years ago, when she broke three ribs. You'd a thought she was dying by the way she carried on. That's when I began to use my 6-inch needle. Works like a charm every time I get a demanding patient. Except on Tammy."

"You'd better go before Miss Demanding has a temper tantrum."

Moonbeam walked up to Thor and inquired, "Sir. Do you want me to have my security keep an eye on Miss Tammy?"

"Yes, thank you."

Cherry suggested, "Hon remember, we have to pay Mr. Tatsuya a visit."

Thor touched his computer watch and stated, "Lacy, have Tammy Lee's 4-star security clearance revoked."

"Sir? You need a good reason to do that."

"I do, Miss Lee has been misusing her security clearance by not following proper protocol."

"Sir, Miss Lee should be brought before a board of Elders in order for you to take away her security clearance."

"Tammy Lee is a loose cannon and I want her tied down. One more thing, have security put a restraining anklet on her so she can't use a portal or the Retrieval Compute."

"She is going to go thermal, when she finds out."

"If she does, have security lock her up. Thor out."

Thor held his wife's hand and said, "We will be taking the blue knows monkey Gumshoe with us. If Mr. Tatsuya is up to something Gumshoe will know it."

In the star car with his wife and the monkey, Thor contacted Rock and said, "This is Star Car One, requesting permission to take off."

"You are clear for departure Sir."

Once the star car had cleared the Rock Pile Asteroid Belt, Thor set a course for the planet, Kylee.

Cherry inquired sweetly, "Thor, Honey. We have been going none stop for the past two weeks. Do you think we can take some time and mix it up before we reach Kylee?"

Thor glanced at his wife with her seat in the full recline position and ordered, "Computer, bring the star car to a complete stop, darken the windows and put on some soft music."

An hour later, Cherry smiled up at her husband and stated, "Do we have to go right this minute? I love it when you are snuggled next to me."

"Okay, I guess we can wait a little longer before we get dressed."

Another hour had passed, Thor continued to the planet Kylee, flew over a mountain five hundred feet high and spotted Mr. Tatsuya's laboratory. Landed the star car in the parking lot of a long flat white building with black type on it that said, Tatsuya Laboratories, the Future Begin Here Thor knocked on the door, and an Asian man, answered the door, saw Thor, and asked, "What do you want now?"

"I want to talk to you about that gun you invented some months ago. You know the one, that I thought was the weapon that liquefied the Hummer-gene's granddaughter, Joanna."

"Every time something happens, you come around and pound on my door trying to accuse me of something. I have nothing to do with all those people being liquefied, now if you will excuse me I have to get back to the work in my lab." and went to close the door. Thor kicked the door open and bellowed, "Not this time. I want to have a closer look at that contraption of yours."

"You can't come in here without a search warrant!" screamed Mr. Tatsuya in protest.

The monkey jumped out of Cherry's arms and scampered up to a futuristic energy rifle mounted on a tripod. Mr. Tatsuya shouted, "Get that monkey away from my invention!"

Thor examined the invention and said, "I see that you have added a few things to it since the last time I saw it. I am confiscating this for further study."

"Don't even think of touching that!" shouted the scientist.

Cherry stuck her energy pistol in the Mr. Tatsuya face and said, "Stay put, if you want to stay healthy."

Thor glared at the scientist and stated, “I’m the Galaxy Sentinel and I am investigating the deaths of hundreds of people whose bodies were liquefied when the atoms of their bodies lost its cohesion.”

Mr. Tatsuya shouted something in Japanese, two muscle-bound Asian men rushed out of a door and charged Thor and Cherry. She stunned one with her energy pistol. While Thor kicked the other one between his pockets, sending him down on his knees in pain. Then landed a hard-right cross knocking him out. Thor turned to Mr. Tatsuya and stated firmly, “I am taking the device to have it thoughtfully examined by a professor I know. If there is a connection between your invention and the spheres in people’s stomachs, I’ll return to arrest you.”

Cherry sprayed the back of Tatsuya’s neck saying, “With the blue tracking compound I just sprayed on you, we will be able to find you no matter where you hide.”

Thor touched his watch and said, “Contact the Professor of Dicapl.”

An elderly man’s head appeared over Thor computer watch. Thor stated, “You’re looking good. How is Hope doing?”

“Oh, fine. What’s up?”

“I need you to check out Mr. Tatsuya’s invention. He says is a medical device, but I am not too sure.”

“I’ll be glad to.” An eight-foot portal opened, Thor pushed Mr. Tatsuya’s invention through and said to Mr. Tatsuya, you will get it back, if you are innocent. Have a wonderful day.”

As they walked to the star car, Cherry stated, “He’s hiding something. Shall we interview his neighbors around the mountain to find out what they know?”

CHAPTER 4

Back to Mr. Tatsuya

Thor drove the star car down the mountain's winding road, to a quiet community just below. Cherry pointed to sign that read, Circle Lane Drive and said, "Let's check out the families here. Seeing it's close to the mountain."

Thor stopped in front of a badge colonial, with an elaborate flower garden around it and rang the doorbell. A woman about four feet tall, clad in burgundy slacks and a white top answered the door, looked up at Thor and asked, "What can I do for You?"

Seeing the sparkle in the woman's eye, Cherry quickly answered, "My husband and I are doing a survey to find out how much interference Mr. Tatsuya's lab is causing here below."

"Come on in. It's about time they sent someone." grumbled the woman, "I've filed a complaint months ago."

"Oh?" inquired Thor, "Can you tell me about the problems that you have been having?"

"It started several months ago, I recorded one of my favorite shows, 'The Young Pioneers,' and got this." The woman led Thor and Cherry into a living room that had a deep pile white rug, light blue drapes with matching furniture picked, up the remote from a mahogany end table and pressed a button. Two black, vertical rods, four feet, long and eight feet apart, slowly lowered from the ceiling.

She inserted a crystal flash drive into a four-inch square black box on the end table and said, "Watch."

The picture of a young woman dressed in a modest, two-piece bathing suit lying on a back-patio sunbathing came into view on the TV. The woman asked sharply, "Does that look like 'The Young Pioneers to you?"

Cherry quickly stated, "That's the Hummer-gene's granddaughter Joanna!" and saw Mr. Tatsuya walked up to Joanna and inquired, "You wanted to talk to me?"

Joanna stood up and said, "You know when we fooled around in the shower two weeks ago? Well you are going to be a father of my baby. But, that's not what I called you over here for. I saw the blueprints for your new invention. You used me, so you could steal the plans to my grandfather's power staff!"

"I have no idea what you are talking about."

"You are not only a thief, but a liar! What do you call that thing you have under that tarp?" Joanna then shouted, "Grandfather! I need to speak to you, now!"

Grey clouds formed nine feet off the patio, an elderly man with long, white hair, down to his ankles, dressed in a long dark blue toga, carrying a twisted and knotted staff in his right hand appeared. He glared at Joanna and roared, "Why have you summoned the Hummer-gene granddaughter of mine?"

"Do you have to be so formal Granddad? I thought I'd tell you before I call the police. Tatsuya stole the plans for your power staff and plans to sell it to the highest bidder."

The Hummer-gene cast a worried glance at Tatsuya, then at Joanna who was staring at her in shock and she asked, "You sold the plans to your staff to Mr. Tatsuya? But why?"

"You won't understand child. I did it for the good, of mankind."

"Cow patties!" screamed Joanna, "All you wanted was the money! I'm gonna report you to your overseer." and entered her house to make the call.

The Hummer-gene twirled his staff over his head and slammed it down on the patio, the walls begin to vibrate an energy beam shot out of his staff and struck Joanna in the back. She let out an agonizing shriek, then exploded into billions of pieces. The Hummer-Gene turned to the scientist and stated, "You have to change the energy pattern on your power cannon or they will know I sold you the blueprints. Don't worry about my granddaughter's death no one will know."

Cherry put her hand to her mouth when she saw Joanna explode saying, "Gross! That was heartless mean and cruel for the Hummer-Gene to granddaughter and I am glad he got what he deserved."

Thor turned to the woman and said, "I need that thumb-drive. It is part of an ongoing murder investigation."

Back in the star car, Cherry questioned, "Hon, how can a grapefruit size sphere with an eggshell thin hull hold all that blue gas under so much pressure without bursting?"

"That is something I have been trying to figure out ever since this whole mess began. But, right now I am going to arrest Mr. Tatsuya as an accessory to Joanna's murder." Thor touched his computer watch and said, "Rock, I need you to send two of your men to meet me on the hill outside Mr. Tatsuya's lab because he is an accessory to Joanna's murder."

Back at Tatsuya's lab, Thor instructed the two burly security guards to stand to one side while he arrested the scientist. Cherry readied her energy pistol as Thor knocked on the door. Mr. Tatsuya answered and said, "You two again. What do you want now?"

Thor's face lost all expression as he stated, Mr. Tatsuya, because of the new evidence surrounding the mutilation of the Hummer-gene's granddaughter, Joanna; "You are hereby retrieved, taken out of society because you are deemed too dangerous to be around any social group. There will be no trial to determine if you are guilty because the evidence has placed you at the scene of the crime"Thor ordered one of the guards to take Mr. Tatsuya back to the Institute and to have the area secure.

In the star, car Cherry suggested, "There is a White Forest Coffee Shop not too far from here. What do you say we stop for a Fuzzy Joe?"

Thor stared at his wife and questioned, "A what?"

"You don't know what a Fuzzy Joe is?"

"An old man with lots of hair?"

Cherry chuckled and said, "It's a cup of coffee and a fuzzy doughnut."

Thor laughed and asked, "What in the world is a fuzzy doughnut?"

"It's a doughnut, with frosting and a few sprigs of cotton candy on top."

"Alright let's go have a Fuzzy Joe."

In the White Forest Cafe, Thor took a swallow of his coffee, stared at his chocolate covered doughnut with white cotton candy on top and muttered "that is so wrong" He looked up at a tall sharply woman entering the crowded coffee shop, with glazed look in her eyes and ordered a cup of coffee. He whispered to Cherry, "get everybody out," than casually walked up to her and questioned, "Is there anything I can do for you ma'am?"

"I have to sit here until four o'clock."

Thor motioned to everyone to leave, Cherry walked up to Thor and reported, "All clear." stared at the doomed woman sitting in a booth sipping her coffee and asked, "Is she going to explode like the others?"

Thor sighed and said, "I'm afraid so, and there is nothing we can do about it."

Cherry glanced at her watch and said, "She has ten minutes left to live and I can't let her go into eternity without Christ."Thor's wife sat next to the woman and asked, "I'm Cherry. Come here often?"

"No, I was walking by and thought I drop in for a cup." the woman placed her hand on her stomach and moaned. Thor knelt by his wife as she asked the woman, "Can I pray for your stomach?"

"Could you please?"

Cherry placed her hand on the woman's belly and felt a grapefruit size orb inside her, glanced at Thor and nodded yes. Then prayed, "LORD, I don't know how to pray for this woman's aliment." Cherry stared at her and asked, "Would you like to give your life to Christ?"

"Yes. I have been away from my Savior way too long." As soon as she recommitted her life to the Lord, she looked at Cherry with her eyes open wide and warned, "You've got to get out of here!" then fell to the floor on her knees with her hands on her stomach groaning in pain. Cherry placed her hand on the woman's back and asked, "What's your name?"

"Zelda. Please get everyone out of here before it is too late!"

"The place is clear of people, Zelda."

Thor tugged on his wife's arm saying, "You've done all you could for her. We have to go."

Just as the door to the White Forest Cafe was closed, they heard Zelda scream, "Jesus, take me home!" then an explosion that splattered her body all over the walls and ceiling, blowing out the windows in the coffee shop. Then, a large cloud of blue vapor rose out the shattered windows towards the unsuspecting crowd that had gathered. Thor shouted, "Get away from here! That's a cloud of deadly gas!"

"Yeah right," replied a stout man paying no attention to Thor's warning and laughing at the others running for their lives. His laughter suddenly tuned into agonizing screams as the blue cloud enveloped him, turning his body into a pool of blue and scarlet ooze.

As the caustic blue cloud drew closer to Thor and Cherry, he frantically searched for a means to escape but they were hemmed in on three sides. Cherry had a death grip on Thor as she closed her eyes waiting for the excruciating pain that would end their lives.

Just then, Prince Blue, a six-foot-tall blue pixie who was ruler of the Will-o'-the-wisps appeared with 24 turquoise military Wisps, ordered his men to fly above the caustic cloud to create a vortex. In minutes the blue cloud was drawn up in the air and dissipated. Blue walked up to Thor, and his wife and asked, "You two alright?"

"Thanks Blue, looks like Cherry, and I caught the brass ring that time around. Another couple of seconds and the First General would have had to find another Galaxy Sentinel.

A green male Will-of-the-wisp clad in white walked up to the large puddle of ooze, that used to be a man, knelt down then ordered his workers to clean it up and stated, "Put the residue from the 2 humans in separate containers.

Prince Blue turned to Thor and said, "There were several attacks in Willow City, but, they failed because of the resiliency of the Will-o'-the-wisps."

Queen Diane of the Tealing Empire flashed in Thor's mind he then heard a banging noise coming from the trunk of the star car. Opened it and found a two-foot-tall Gideon Bear, clad in a blue and gold kimono with his katana strapped to his back. Thor questioned, "You mind telling me, why you decided to stowaway in my trunk Gidester?"

Gideon flipped forward, landed on Thor's left shoulder, and slowly scanned the crowd of onlookers, with his blade in his paw. Spotted a tall thin man, with short brown hair, dressed in blue pants and a white shirt. Gideon jumped off Thor's shoulder, quickly waddled up to the man, bounced off a woman's hip, landed on the man's shoulder and stuck his sword against his throat. Thor approached the suspect Gideon had picked out as the man growled, "Get that thing off me, or I will sue you for everything you have."

"I did a quick scan of you and found traces of the dead woman's DNA. Care to explain, that?"

The man threw Gideon off his shoulders, knocked Thor to the ground, spun around and sprinted away before Thor had a chance to recover.

The bear handed Thor a piece of artificial skin then pointed to the suspect. Thor placed it in a small plastic bag, thanked the bear then shook Prince Blue's hand for his assistance and said, "Come on Cherry, we have to go to Nautikos City on the moon of the dark planet and check on Diane to see how the Tealing Empire is doing."

An hour and twenty minutes later, Thor flew over Nautikos, the capital of the Tealing Empire, a city of white buildings with gold roofs and landed by the giant statue of the Phoenix bird. He contacted Queen Diane and inquired, "Cherry and I just dropped by to see how things are going. Have you had any Blue Scarlet attacks?"

"I am so glad you two are here, I have had a few scarlet attacks, but my main problem is a radical group that is terrorizing the people."

"Be there in a few minutes. Thor out."

Thor drove his vehicle through the gray paved streets up to the twelve-foot-high, garnet wall with its fancy wrought iron gate. The gates opened by themselves and Thor parked his car on the marble parade ground. Queen Diane, a tall woman with wavy blond hair, clad in her royal attire, greeted Thor and his wife. Her eyes fell on Gideon and Gumshoe and exclaimed, "Oh how cunning! Are they your pets?"

Thor picked up the bear and said, "This is Gideon, The Avenging Bear, the best swordsman in the galaxy and this is Gumshoe who loves emergency ration bars and has a nose for trouble. Where is your husband, Dave?"

"He is presently arguing with the general of my military about how to defeat these terrorists."

"Would Dave mind if I put my two cents in?"

"Go ahead. Maybe you can break the stalemate."

Thor kissed his wife goodbye and sauntered off to locate Dave. Five minutes later he entered a room with mahogany carved walls and found a tall, lanky man with short, light brown hair in an intense argument with a tall well-built man clad in a red and blue dress military uniform. Thor cleared his throat and stated, "Maybe I can shed some light on your conundrum."

The General quickly turned, faced Thor, and barked, "Who the devil are you and how did you get in here?"

"I am the Galaxy Sentinel and General your plan to combat the terrorist with high energy weapons is correct. But, not in this case. If I may assume the terrorist have all the modern technology, then, the only choice of weapons are Gatling guns, Ak-47s and rocket launchers with a few archers for good measure."

"Are you nuts? For the past two days, I have been trying to tell Dave, shooting piece of lead at someone won't work." bellowed a frustrated General.

"On the contrary general, they will work. The energy shields today are great for protecting against an energy cannon, but, can't detect a junk of led or a rocket."

The general stared at Thor in silence for fifteen seconds pondering his statement then said, "I never thought of that. It just may work. Okay, where do I get my hand on weapons like that?"

"How much do you need? Better yet. Let me surprise you. Thor touched his computer watch and said, "Sal old buddy, I need you to send me some weapons."

"Okay who do you want to beat the crap out of now?"

"A bunch of terrorist, I need 6 tanks, 50 dozen cases of grenade launchers, 300 AK-47s and 5 Gatling guns with plenty of ammo and 200 dozen cases of hand-grenades. How soon can you get it here?"

"Give me a day or two."

CHAPTER 5

Fritz

The General slued Thor and left, Widget A large gray mouse with transparent wings, that changes color with his emotions, entered the room on its hind quarters and up to Thor and asked, "Do you know a pudgy man with red hair, bald on top, carries a javelin and goes by the name of Admiral Sam the Stout?"

"Sure do, send him in."

"Sam walked in and stated, "Sal just told me that you ordered enough weapons to start a small war. What gives?"

"There is a bunch of radicals in the city trying to cause trouble and the only way to stop them is with Earth style artillery."

"In other words, you want to pound the snot out of them."

"Pretty much."

"Hey, do they have a coffee shop somewhere in this city?"

"Why don't we mix business with pleasure and talk to the people. Maybe we can find out where their hideout is." suggested Thor.

"Sounds like a plan to me. Let's go."

Thor located Dave in the castle and asked for a list of bars and coffee shops. Dave questioned, "Going slumming?"

"Nope, just want to pump the people for information hopefully we can discover where those Creeps are hiding. Dave. Tell my wife I'll see her in a few hours. Come on Sam we have work to do."

A few blocks south of the palace gates, Thor rented a blue hover platform with red railing around it. Sam stated, "You drive, while I watch for whomever."

A short distance down the street, Sam pointed to a middle-aged woman being harassed by a tall well-dressed man in his thirties. Thor stopped the hover platform, approached the woman, and asked, "Is there anything my friend and I can do to help?"

"Butt out mister, this is none of your business." stated the man

"Since there are no police around to intervene, it is our business. Now, what is the problem, ma'am?"

The man glared at Thor and muttered, "You Schwachsinnige." and walked away.

Thor stared at the man and muttered, "You know Sam. I think he just insulted us."

"I don't think, I know he just insulted us. The guy just called us morons in German. Ma'am is there anything we can do for you?"

"No. I am too upset to talk."

"Can you tell me what the conversation was all about?"

"He is talking against the Queen. Now, if you will excuse me, I have to meet my husband."

Thor stated, "Hop on blue hover platform Sam, I want to have a few words with Fritz."

Thor caught up with the man, swerved the platform so it blocked his path. Jumped over the railing, grabbed the man by his arm and stated, "If you are going to call me a moron do it in English. Now, what do you have against her Highness?"

The man straightened his shoulders and said, "Unhand me. I am Hadulfo Beckenbauer the famous artist."

"I don't care who you are. You don't go around bothering the Queen's subjects and get away with it. Now, assume the position."

"This is an outrage!"

Mr. Beckenbauer emptied his pockets, faced the platform, took hold of it, and spread his legs. Sam picked up his digital wallet, entered a code and brought up all the information. Sam stated, "Our friend here is a painter like he says. Oh, this is interesting,

Hadulfo. Mr. Beckenbaue can I call you Hadulfo?" Explain to Thor and me why there is several large amounts of money being deposited then withdrawn? Like a week ago, there was seventy-five thousand dollars deposited into your account and two days later it is withdrawn. Care to explain?"

"I don't have to tell you anything until I speak to my lawyer."

Thor picked up a small vial of fine grey powder from Hadulfo's things and asked, "You mind telling me what this is?"

"I don't have to tell you anything until I speak to my lawyer." repeated the man.

"Not going to happen Mr. Hadulfo, I am the Galaxy Sentinel, and you are hereby retrieved, removed from society until I deem you fit to return. Sam, call the Institute security and have him taken away." Thor stared at the vial of gray powder and said, "I am going to hold onto this for now."

Sam turned to Thor and stated, "I think we are on to something. Let's try that bar. Over there, maybe we will strike gold."

"You mean that dive called, 'The Pit.'?" inquired Sam, "Looks like loads of fun. After you."

Inside the dark, smoke filled bar, sat the dregs of the galaxy. Few paid any attention to Thor and Sam as they entered. Sam approached the bartender and inquired, "Has anyone been in here speaking German?"

"There was one man in here just a few minutes ago talking to that to blond man sitting at the table alone."

Thor and Sam walked to the table, sat down with the blond man and Thor asked, "You always come here when you are planning to overthrow the government?"

The man took a swallow of his beer, glanced at Thor than at Sam and stared at the door. Sam slowly reached down, took hold of his metal club, ready to expand it into a javelin. The man quickly flipped the table over and made a mad dash for the door.

Sam sprang to his feet extended his javelin and threw it striking the man in his back, he glanced down at the point of the javelin sticking out of his chest, reached for the door, then fell to the floor, dead. Sam removed his javelin, turned the man over and checked his pockets for his ID. But found a vial of grey dust and a blank digital wallet, in his pocket. Sam glanced at it, handed to Thor, and said, "Ever see one of these?"

"Yes. He was an Inadvisable. Someone who doesn't have an identity."

"In other words, a trained assassin."

"More like an expendable killer. A man was cloned for the sole purpose of killing someone, when his assignment is complete, he just up and dies."

Two police officers rushed up, one slammed Thor against the building, Sam stuck his Javelin under the chin of the other officer and ordered, "Tell your partner to back off, or I will shove it right through your head."

The officer ordered, "Let him go Mike."

Once Thor was released, he stated, "I see you two haven't done your homework. I'm the Galaxy Sentinel and this is Admiral Sam the Stout. The one you see on the ground was a hired killer."

"Can you prove that?" questioned one officer.

Thor handed him the dead man's digital wallet and stated, "As you can see, he has no ID but an access code in his digital wallet, so he can withdraw whatever he wants from any bank in the Alliance."

"That doesn't give you the right to murder him in cold blood and tell your fat friend to lose the spear."

"As the Galaxy Sentinel, I have the authority to use deadly force if I think it is necessary."

A short time later, 4 yellow police cars screeched to a halt carrying 15 heavily armed officers and surrounded them with weapons drawn. One shouted, "Let the hostages go!"

Sam glanced at Thor and stated, "Seven to one, that's just about right."

Thor took the officers energy weapon, tossed one to Sam saying, "Tie them up in the bar and had everyone get down on the floor. Thor then shouted, "I am the Galaxy Sentinel visiting her Highness, the Queen, concerning the Blue Scarlet attacks! If you don't believe me, call her!"

Three policemen crept in the back door of the bar to overtake Sam and release the so-called hostages. Sam caught the officers and threw them outside the front door starting a free for all in the bar. The other officers outside, rushed in to assist creating a bigger problem. Three minutes into the fight, Thor's computer phone rang, he answered it and said, "Rock, can I get back to you in a few? I am rather busy right now. Sam, you've got one coming up on your back! Talk to you later."

Thirty seconds later, a portal opened, and three dozen Institute security rushed through and had everything under control. Thor turned to Rock and asked, "Now, what was it that you wanted?"

"You know those 4 she-devil sprites that Moonbeam inducted into the sprite security? Moonbeam has them on shark patrol on Smile Lake beach."

Thor chuckled and said, "There are no sharks in Smile Lake. They must have done something for Moonbeam to do something to them like that. Oh, while you are here, take that dead man back to Chrissy. I need to know who he is. Sam and I can handle things here."

Once Rock and the security team left, Thor contacted the palace and said, "Dave, I need two dozen castle guards to the Pit, Now."

With the bar under control the captain of the castle guard turned to Thor and inquired, "You two need a lift back?"

"Thanks, but no thanks we have a hover transport platform, and thanks for the assist."

"I've been looking for a reason to shut this place down for months. See you guys back at the castle."

Eager for more action, Sam turned to Thor and asked, "You want to ask a few more questions in another bar and start a riot?"

"No." Thor stared at his friend and asked. "Do you normally block a left hook with your face? That right eye of yours looks nasty."

"It was either that or get it in the stomach from the guy with the broken bottle in his hand."

Back at the castle, Cherry met the two men and exclaimed, "Good Lord! What happened to you two? Get run over by a stampede of elephants. You two look like crap."

"We had a disagreement with a few men in a bar, no big deal." stated Thor.

"Plus, half the city's police force." added Sam, "I think I'm gonna look for a raw steak for my eye. See you later Thor."

In their luxurious blue bedroom, with its deep pile rug. Cherry stated, "Thor, the first thing you are going to do is take a shower. Then you are going to lay on the bed, so I take care of that sore back of yours."

"My back feels fine." stated Thor, trying not to wince from the pain.

"Don't give me that macho routine. I can tell your back is hurting just by the way you are walking."

After Thor's shower, Cherry spread a bath towel on the bed and ordered, "Lose the towel and lay on your stomach so can treat you."

Cherry put on a pair of latex gloves, opened a large blue with white print package and removed a fabric, soaked in a red sticky substance. Then spread it on Thor's back; from his shoulders to his hips then smoothed it out. After, she covered Thor with a plastic sheet and a blanket stating, "The sticky sheet I put on your back should heat up in a minute and you are to lay in that position for an hour."

"I can't lay here like this." protested Thor, "I have things to do."

"You will stay there like that until I say otherwise. I will not have my husband laid up with a bad back. Now, give me a minute and I will join you."

The next morning, Thor rose from the bed and moaned, "Cherry can you get this thing off my back?"

Cherry groaned, "It's six in the morning Hon. Come back to bed."

"Can't. I have things to do. Now give me a hand with this will ya."

"Oh alright." Cherry took hold of the sticky sheet she placed on his back, but it wouldn't come off. She then stated, "I guess you were not to leave it on all night. Let me get the package. Maybe it will tell me how to get off." Cherry read the package and said, "Ah, you have to run warm water over it. Give me a minute and I'll join you in the shower."

Thor walked in the blue and white tiled bathroom and opened the clear crystalline shower door and studied the large shower shaped like a baseball diamond. Cherry walked up behind him with a white towel wrapped around her, saying, "Come on Tiger let's get this thing off you." She threw her towel on the toilet and entered the shower with her husband.

An hour later, Thor walked out of the bathroom smiling with his wife and said, "I didn't know you would be that kittenish this early in the morning."

A soft knock came at the door, Cherry growled as Thor went to answer it, "Wait till I put something on first!" as she jumped on the bed and quickly pulled the covers over her grumbling, "Thor Stromburg, you are impossible!"

Thor stood behind the door, opened it just enough to see who it was. Gideon Bear waddled in, glared up at Thor with his paws on his hips.

"It's not my fault you stayed up all night Squirt." stated Thor, staring at the irate bear. So, what is on your mind Gidester?"

The bear pointed to the door then to Cherry. Thor thought for a moment then asked, "Is there is a woman in trouble?"

Gideon nodded head yes.

"Give me a minute to put some clothes on and I'll follow you."

Dressed, Thor put the blue bear on his shoulder, kissed Cherry and went out the door. The bear lead Thor to the East Courtyard that was paved with stones and dotted with shade trees.

Sitting on a bench under a tree, was a young sprite sitting perfectly still clad in skimpy attire with long light brown hair. Thor approached the sprite, knelt in front of her and asked, "Are you alright?"

The sprite stayed motionless as she stared straight ahead. Cherry knelt next to Thor, put her hand on the sprite's knee and asked, "Would you like a cup of hot tea?"

Gideon pointed his katana at the sprite's left leg and sliced it open. Thor shouted, "That was uncalled for Mister!"

Cherry examined the wound and said, "She's not real. Look." Cherry pulled some plant fibers out of the wound and said in amazement, "She is a plant. But How?"

"I can tell you that." stated a castle guard from behind them, "She is a Replica of the real sprite put there by the 12. Please stand back she may go off at any moment." The guard blew a high-pitched whistle and a moments later, 6 men dressed in black and yellow has-mat suits, with sprayer canisters strapped to their backs rushed up to the sprite, placed a clear blast proof shield around her, then stood ready. A minute later, a loud bang shook the courtyard sending parts of the imitation sprite flying everywhere. Ushering forth a giant caustic blue cloud that threatened to dissolve everything in its path. The 6 men quickly surrounded the cloud and sprayed it with a dark gray dust. Turning it into a swirling mass of blue and scarlet, before fading into nothing. Thor walked up to one of the men and inquired, "What was that you just sprayed on the cloud to neutralize it?"

"All I know it is some kind of spore found in the Dead Forest. Now, if you will excuse me, we have a mess to clean up."

Cherry glanced at her watch and said, "We better hoof it if we want to eat this morning."

CHAPTER 6

Welcome to The Planet, Montros

Cherry, Thor, and Sam entered the Queen's stylish, living quarters and found Queen Diane clad in jeans and a short-sleeved top, busy in the kitchen, cooking the morning meal. Cherry scanned all the Earth's appliances in the kitchen, then carefully examined the electric range and commented, "For a Queen, you sure don't act like one. I would never store my food in a fridge, because the food would go bad too fast."

"I lived on Earth for years before I became Queen and got use to their way of living. What would you like to drink with your breakfast; coffee, tea, milk, juice?"

Cherry stared at Diane and questioned,"Breakfast? What's that?"

"The first meal of the day. It breaks the nightly fast. Or what they call it here, the morning meal."

"Oh, okay Coffee."

At the table, Thor handed Dave, the vial of gray powder and asked, "What do you make of this?"

"Some twenty-five miles to the north of here lies a valley of soft, black humus. In it grows a forest of tall, dark grey, spores resembling thirty-foot trees. Ergo, the Dead Forest. It's the spores from those trees we use to combat the blue acid cloud attacks that you refer to as Blue Scarlet. Where did you get that tube of spores from?"

"Sam and I took down to Germans that were carrying these vials."

"They must be trying to find a way to create a super acid that will be impervious to the spores."

"Who are they?" questioned Thor.

"They are men who serve 'The 12.' and I am surprise that you were able to defeat them. Each member is an expert in the Martial Arts with catlike reflexes."

Sam took a swallow of his coffee and asked, "I was a little late for the action in the East Courtyard this morning, but what is a Replica?"

"That's easy. The Replicas are plants resembling human beings. Diane has one of us in her garden. Come, I'll show you."

Dave led Thor, Sam, and Cherry through their living quarters to their private garden in the back. Then explained, "My wife has flowers and shrubs from all over the galaxy." Dave paused by two replicas in the middle of the garden that resembled Dave and his wife. And stated, "Somewhere in the Dead Forest is an oasis of lush, green vegetation, in the center is an amazing large pool of dark green sludge. The Tealing Scientist have been trying for years to figure out its chemical mixture but can't."

"What so amazing about it?" Inquired Sam.

"You see those reproductions of Diane and me. We touched the slime and that what grew out of it in a few days."

"Will it droop?"

"Nope, all that it needs to be done is to put the replicas on bare ground and water it. The replica will send roots into the ground and it last forever. But, the down side if it. The 12 are using the sludge to reproduce Replicas to help carry out their acid attacks."

"In other words, they have control over the green goo in the Dead Forest."

"That isn't the worst of it. Last week, they captured twelve of the Palace's Women Scouts and threatened to kill them if we attempt a rescue."

"Are you sure that The Dreaded 12 have the women?" inquired Cherry.

The plant Replica that blew up a short while ago was one of the sprite scouts."

"Have you tried to rescue the women?" inquired Thor.

"Yes, and they killed one of the women and sent her body to the palace."

Thor thought for a minute, then asked, "When were you and Queen Diane going to let the rest of the Alliance know that the 12 are behind these attacks and when we're going to let us know about neutralizer for the Blue Scarlet?"

"Two weeks ago, my head scientist found a way to duplicate the gray spores. But this morning was the first chance we had to test it out."

"How did you know the spores would work to begin with?"

"Some of the palace guards were in the Dead Forest on maneuvers when a Bobcat wandered up and lay by a spore tree. The cat then exploded releasing the blue acid cloud, also shattering a nearby spore Tree. The spores from the tree immediately attacked the acid cloud and turned the cloud to crimson.

By now, my scientists should have contacted Harry, the first General, about the good news."

"Sam, Gidester and I should be able rescue your scouts."

Sam chuckled and said, "They'll never know what hit them."

I can't let you go after them. I don't want those dead women on my conscience."

Thor reassured Dave, "We can get in and out without being detected."

"How can you do when my trained men could not do it?"

"I have Gideon, the Avenging Bear. A two-foot-tall, blue Three-Dimensional Particle Acceleration bear. Which can't be picked up by any sensor."

"Well, alright. But I will hold you personality responsible if any of those women are killed."

The Queen approached her husband and said, "Farmer Alwin who lives in the Agatharchides Valley is complaining about being attacked by the Gila Monster again."

"Diane, I have sent my guards out there two dozen times looking for the fictitious lizard and all they found was nothing. I am not going to send my men out on another fool's errand."

Sam stated, "Thor and I will take care of that pokey venomous lizards. How big can it be? Two feet long?"

Dave gazed at Thor and stated, "The Agatharchides Valley is twelve miles east of here. Good luck."

Sam asked, "Thor, did you bring our cloaks and hats? We'll need them, if we are going to sneak up on, The 12."

"They are in the trunk of the star car, we head out first thing in the morning to take care of a little lizard problem, then we go after the 12."

Diane approached Thor and said, "There is a call on the video phone. You can take it in the den."

Thor sat in front of the video phone, saw Moonbeam, and asked, "What's up?"

"I just wanted to give you an update on the progress of the tram tunnel. We "We have bored down nine hundred feet and will begin to enlarge the cavern where the station will be built tomorrow."

"Why bore down nine hundred feet?"

"The Institute sits on top of Mount Baldwin, some seven hundred feet above Smile Lake. We have to drill below the beach in order to build the second tram station."

"When do you think, you will reach the beach?"

"With the way, the boring is proceeding, we should reach the beach in a week's time. Oh, the rest of the building materiel will arrive tomorrow."

"How are those four She devils: Constance, Mimi, Darlene, and Susanna, doing?"

"Constance, Darlene and Susanna, are still pulling pranks on people. Rose was walking down the jungle path from the housing project to the Institute in a nice white dress, when her foot was snared by a rope and was hoisted up in a tree. Those she devils jumped out from a nearby bush and sprayed her with blue paint."

Thor inquired, "What is it that you are not telling me?"

"You see Sir. A few of the ladies on the staff found out and Cathy, Missy and Lacy, dumped ten gallons of black-strap molasses and feathers all over them."

"I assume the whole thing was a setup to teach those she-devils a lesson and sprite Mimi has stopped hanging around them."

"She has been a great help, especially with Mary Bell's prayer and support group. Oh, Rock wants to say a few words."

Rock sat in front of the video phone and reported, "I had to suspend swimming at Smile Lake until the underwater protective netting is put in place, because of fresh water shark sightings."

"Have you organized a search party to look for the sharks?"

"Already have Sir. Abbie, Tippy and some of the sprite security scouring the lake now."

"Good. Keep me posted on situation. Thor out."

Dave walked up to Thor and said, "I need you to come with me."

Thor kissed his wife and said, "I don't know when I will be back."

Outside the castle, Dave rushed Thor in a long black hover limo and ordered, "Driver, take us to the building."

After going down one side street after another, the car came to a stop in front of an old deserted crumbling factory with row after row of square cement columns. Dave leaned forward and said, "Driver, don't wait for us." stepped out of the limo and said, "Thor, you will follow me."

"You wanna tell me what's going on?"

Dave remained quiet as he entered the rubble strewn building, passing one row of columns after another until he came to a column with two half demolished walls. Dave approached one wall, pressed a square, silver knob opening a portal doorway next to it, then stated, "After you."

"You mind telling me what's this is all about?"

"In time, but you must trust me on this."

Thor entered the shimmering doorway and found himself in a shabby ten by ten room with a grungy metal slot one wall. Dave walked up to the slot, and dropped a thick octagon shaped piece of metal in it. A man entered the room, gave Dave an octagon piece of metal and said, "Glad to see you again Dave. Who do we have here?"

"This is Thor Manning Stromburg, AKA, the Galaxy Sentinel."

The man turned to Thor and said, "Welcome to the planet Montros. I am Goth, will you please follow me to the map room."

In the map room, Goth stood at the end of a long narrow smooth table, Thor stood on the right and Dave on the left. Goth touched the table and a long map appeared with rugged terrain. Goth recited a long list of cities ending in ous, then pointed to the two major cities in bold, black type, Debous on the upper right and Batra down a bit on the left and stated, "This is where I am having trouble with aliens, disguising themselves as human and steal a dead human's identity. I want you to be the Ambassador to Montros. I will pay you ten thousand Druxes a month to round up these renegades and send them back to Montros, where I will deal with them."

Thor stared at Goth and said, "But you are human in every sense of the word."

"No, I am not. I am a Montronian. Observe." Goth's appearance suddenly blurred then and alien with flesh tone skin, long triangle shaped head, long ears, bulging eyes, a long nose and a slit for a mouth, stared at Thor. He extended his long thin arm towards Thor with a ruby pen in his boney fingers and stated, "I have uploaded an app to your computer watch that will cause it to vibrate when you are near a Montronian. Use this ruby pen to send the renegades back to Montros for judgment."

Thor questioned, "What makes you think that I am qualified for the job?"

You are the Galaxy Sentinel, are you not? Then you are the only one in the galaxy that can do the job. Do you accept?"

Thor took the ruby pen and said, "I accept."

"Give me your digital wallet so I can transfer twenty thousand Druxes into your account. The extra money is to help you get started in your new job."

Once the money was in Thor's account, Goth stated, "I will send you to the city of Batra on Montros, so you can get a feel of things. The Lord Jesus be with you."

On the bustling city streets of Batra on the planet Montros, Thor stared at the store fronts made of black onyx. Spotted something that looked like a diner, entered, sat at the counter, and asked, "What do you have that's hot to drink?"

The alien waiter behind the counter put a gray metal glass in front of Thor, poured a hot brown liquid in it saying, "Mister. All we here serve is goheeh. Would you like something to eat with that?"

Thor picked up a flat piece of wood with scribbling on it then made as if he could not see to read. The waiter huffed and said, "How about the Batra Special?"

"Sounds good." Thor placed his nose over his glass and muttered, "It smells like coffee."

The waiter sat a yellow glass plate down in front of Thor resembling a cheeseburger deluxe and stated, "Hey buddy, if you are going to look like a human, I'd pick another disguise other than the Galaxy Sentinel. Here is the address of someone who can help you with a fresh look and it will only cost you a few thousand Druxes. When you walk in just asked the little man behind the counter, "What does the face of evil look like today? He will set you up with new features. Good luck buddy and the meal is on me."

Several miles from the city, Thor sauntered in a freestanding gray stone building in the middle of a field of tall green grass. Entered and discovered it was a curio shop. He stared at the Montronian midget and asked him, "What does the face of evil look like today?"

"Follow me into the back and I will show you." The midget put a closed sign on the door and led Thor into the back room and told him to sit in the chair by an old antique desk. He held a ruler up to Thor's face saying they call me 'The Face Master.' By the way, who did your reproduction? It's horrible. You look nothing like the Galaxy Sentinel. If that is who you are trying to mimic."

"It was an attempt." muttered Thor.

"Okay, this is how it works. You pay me two thousand Druxes to correct the lousy job the previous guy did on you."

Thor paid The Face Master the money and he was led into a large room full of electronic equipment. Thor noticed a wall full of photos to his right and asked, "Who are these?"

Those are all my master pieces or what the Montronian call Renegades. What do you think?"

Thor paused at a photo of Mr. Hadulfo Beckenbauer and inquired, "Did you create a new look for him too?"

"Sure did. He came in six months ago and had me turn him into German. Go figure."

Thor smiled at the Face Master and stated, "I am not a Montronian. I'm the Galaxy Sentinel and the Ambassador to Montros. You my alien friend, are out of business." and Thor pointed the ruby pen at the Face Master and squeezed, ushering two alien police clad in red with blue trim uniforms. They glanced around the room, grabbed the midget, said, "So long." and vanished.

Before Thor could reach the exit door, a dozen alien men burst through brandishing Earth style automatic weapons and opened fire spraying the room with lead. Thor leaped behind a piece of equipment and hunkered down until he saw his chance. Then, swiftly sprang to his feet, grabbed an alien, by his head, gave it a quick twist and snapped his neck. With the dead alien's gun in hand, Thor returned fire taking out several aliens before jumping down a large pipe in the floor that deposited him in a sizable empty room. Thor stuck his gun in the pipe and emptied the ammo clip. A minute later, seven alien bodies, tumbled out on the floor riddled with bullet holes.

Thor dropped the gun, turned, and made his way back to the long black hover limo waiting for him outside the abandoned, rubble strewn building.

CHAPTER 7

The Agatharchides Valley

Back at the Castile that evening Thor, Cherry, and Sam sat in the Queens private study trying to make scene of the Blue Scarlet attacks. Thor reported, "I am now the Ambassador to the planet Montros and found out that the 12 are not Germans, but aliens made to look human. Who are controlled by the head honcho?"

Sam asked, "Do you still think Mr. Tatsuya is the man behind the 12? He has the knowledge to create something like that blue cloud of acid and has the means to deliver it."

Cherry stated, "I think we can rule out the unknown chemical that breaks down the molecular cohesion in the body since the spores counteract the blue cloud."

Thor said, "We don't know the chemical compassion of the spores or the blue cloud, so we can't rule out the spores just yet. There may be a chemical in the spores that stabilizes the molecular cohesion."

Cherry questioned, "What I like to know is. How can all that gas come out of a container the size of a grapefruit? The shell is thin, so it can' withstand a lot of internal pressure!"

Sam glanced at Cherry and stated, "Could they have filled the sphere with a solution, then put in a time delayed catalyst. When the two mix, it creates gaseous cloud with extreme pressure violently tearing the victim apart releasing the gas."

Thor suggested, "We can be here all day speculating on how it is done. Let's just be thankful that we have something to battle it with."

Sam questioned, "How are we going to know who the alien is disguised as a human?"

"I have an app in my watch that will buzz when it picks up a Montronian as a human."

"Do you think you can upload it to my computer watch?"

"Okay, I'll upload the program to you and my wife. That's all."

A palace guard hollered from the doorway, "There's trouble in the throne room!"

Thor raced to the throne room with Sam, and Cherry but was stopped at the door by the guards. Thor stared at Queen Diane frozen on her throne with a replica standing ten feet in front of her. Thor asked the guard, "What's wrong?"

"That is a replica of one of the Queens maids and has a motion sensor attached to it bomb. If the she moves, the bomb will take out half the throne room along with the Queen."

"What about opening a portal underneath the replicate and dropping it into the next century?"

"I already tried that Sir. I can't get a gateway to stabilize."

"Get me two 8-foot-long poles, two white bed sheets and some tape."

Ten minutes later, the guard handed Thor what he asked for and questioned, "Now what?"

Thor tapped the bed sheets to the two pols, tucked the tape in his pocket and instructed, "Sam hold the sheet up in front of you and slowly walk to the replicate. When we get there, you maneuver to the front of the figure keeping the sheet between you and the replicate." Thor handed the guard the roll of tape and said, "Once we have the replicate covered, I need you to tape it up."

Ten minutes later the Queen was safe, and bomb was deposed, Thor shook Sam's hand saying, "Thanks. I guess we will have to tackle that Gila monster tomorrow."

In his bedroom, Thor stretched out on the bed and was about close his eyes when he heard his wife, "Thor, is that you?"

"Yeah Hon, what's up?"

"I'm kinda stuck."

Thor casually walked in the bathroom and found his wife wrapped in a bath towel and questioned, "What's the problem? Forgot how to take off a bath towel? It's easy, just let go of the two ends and it will fall to the floor."

Cherry sobbed, "I used one of those sticky heat things for my back than wrapped myself in a bath towel and fell asleep. Now the towel is stuck to the heat wrap and the wrap is stuck to me."

Thor stepped behind his wife and said, "Cherry let go of the towel and hold on to something."

"You are not going to do what I think you are going to do."

"Just hold on to something."

Cherry griped the towel bar and cringed saying, "Okay go ahead. Do it."

Cherry let go a bloodcurdling scream as Thor quickly ripped the sticky heating pad off her back. He then held his sobbing wife in his arms saying, "Sorry Sweetheart that was the only way I could think of getting it off you. How's your back feeling?"

"Sore! What do you think?"

"Lie on the bed and I will rub something on your back to ease the pain."

The next morning Thor approached Dave and said, "We need to inspect the plaice guards for a mole."

"Sounds like Pan. I'll have the men standing in formation in ten minutes."

A brief time later, Sam with his javelin in his hand, and Thor next to him slowly walked down the long line of men inspecting every part of their uniform. When Thor was finished, he stood in front of a tall muscular man and hollered, "Dismissed! All but you. I was impressed with your performance in the East Court yard the other day and the way you handled yourself when the Queen's life was in jeopardy." Thor thought for a moment then asked, "I didn't get your name corporal."

"Maze, Sir."

"Maze. I need you to help me solve a puzzle. This word W-A-S is often mispronounced. How would you say it?"

"That is easy Sir it's pronounced, wiss."

Thor got in Maze's face and said, "You're a renegade. Only Montronian mispronunciation the word, was. Why are you trying to kill Queen Diane? Are you part of the 12?"

Maze grabbed Thor, flipped him to the ground and sprinted across the courtyard. Sam cocked his arm and let his javelin fly, striking Maze between his shoulder blades.

Thor, Sam, and Dave walked up to Maze lying on the ground, Sam yanked his spear out and asked, "Why?"

"Because we can." moaned Maze as his body quickly transformed back into his alien form and died." Dave stared at the dead alien an inquired, "How did you know he wasn't human?"

Thor stared at Dave and pondered whether he should tell him. Then asked, "Does Ambassador to an alien world mean anything?"

"Oh yeah. Volumes." Are you going to give up being the Galaxy Sentinel?"

"No. I'll delegate that position to someone who can handle the job. Concerning the Montronians disguised as humans. Any word that has the letters 'AS' in it, they pronounce is as 'IS'."

"Breakfast is getting cold." stated Dave.

Sam stared at Dave and inquired, "Breakfast? What in the world is that?"

"You know the first meal of the day that breaks your nightly fast."

"Oh. You mean the morning meal. Why didn't you say so? Let's eat."

After, Thor scoped up Gideon, put him on his shoulder, kissed his wife, picked up his backpack and headed out of the castle with Sam to kill the Gila Monster.

That evening, Thor walked out of the woods, on the south side of a lush narrow valley below with Sam and saw a quiet river running through it. Thor, and turned left, followed the touch lit path down the mountain side, through old stone arches and a tunnel carved out by hand into the village below.

Once they, crossed the stone bridge and entered a village teeming with people selling their wares. Sam spotted a quaint restaurant and suggested, "Shall we."

In the restaurant, a short stout man escorted them to a booth and said, "Your Waitress will be here in just a few minutes. Would you like something to drink while you are waiting?"

"Two coffees please." stated Sam.

A young woman in her mid-twenties clad in a blue and yellow skirt and blouse approached the booth and asked, "I'm Nina. What do you gentleman want?"

Thor's watch buzzed signaling that the woman was a renegade. Thor took out his ruby red pen, pointed it at her to send her back to Montros for trial.

The waitress froze in fear and pleaded, "Please don't send me back."

"Give me one reason why I shouldn't."

"I have a physical defect and I would be treated is an outcast because my people are perfectionist, and despising anyone who is flawed."

Just then, a tall rugged man approached the waitress carrying a baby and gave her a kiss. The waitress stated, "I'll be off in a few minutes."

Her husband glanced at his wife then at Thor and asked, "What did he do to you?"

Nina turned to her husband Virge and said, "He's here to send us back to Montros."

Thor smiled and said, "As far as I am concern, there are no renegades in this valley. My friend and I are here to kill a Gila Monster."

"Thank you, Sir. Why don't you stay with Nina and me for the night? But how did you know who we were?"

"Simple Virge, you pronounced the word outcast when you should have said outcast. All the words that have 'AS in them, you Montronians pronounce as 'IS.' clean up your English and you will be good to go."

Nina turned to her husband, took her daughter from him and said, "I'll be ready to go as soon as I serve these gentlemen, Sweetheart"

"Why don't we invite them home for supper instead?"

Nina turned to Sam and asked, "You gents like stew?"

"Love it. Lead the way." stated Sam.

Virge, Thor, and Sam walked to a the north side of the valley, to a one-story chestnut brown, house with a slanted flat roof and a spacious yard.

Sam scanned Virge's foot high lawn and inquired, "You have a mower? I'll take care of your grass for you."

"It broke last month and haven't the time to fix it."

"Leave that up to me." answered Sam and trotted off.

After supper, Thor inquired, "Would you happen to know of a chicken farmer having trouble with a Gila Monster lizard?"

Virge thought for a moment then stated, "That would be Alwin's farm. But there hasn't been any kind of lizards in the Agatharchides Valley that I can remember. Who told you that?"

The Queen has been getting complaints from a farmer by the name of Alwin Castaneda."

"Him. He has a spread down by the river. Why don't you two stay the night and leave in the morning?"

The next morning at Mr. Castaneda's farm, Thor spotter a tall man coming out of a chicken-coop greeted him and stated, "The Queen tells me that you are having trouble with a Gila Monster."

The man vigorously shook Thor's saying, "I'm Alwin and boy am I ever glad to see you. That thing had been eating my checker eggs every morning. I hope you brought an energy cannon to take care of the beast."

Sam glanced at Alwin and muttered, "Energy cannon? Why would you need a cannon for a lizard that is only two feet long?"

Alwin moaned and stated, "Gentleman add another twenty-nine more feet to that and you will have the size of my problem."

"A Gila Monster, some thirty feet long? Are you serious?"

A Leprechaun suddenly approached Thor clad in green shorts and a white shirt grumbled, "Leaving me out of all the fun again."

Thor hollered, "Patrick, Pixy! Where did you guys come from and how did you know I was here?"

"I have me ways. Now, what about this thirty-foot lizard?"

Alwin stared at the three men in front of him and suggested, "Let's go inside where it's cooler, then we can discuss this further over a tall glass of Dicapl Nectar."

Inside, Pixy carefully studied the light green wallpaper with large white fern print, the comfortable red chair and the forest green sofa and stated, "Alwin, I take it you've been to Earth."

"Not many people notice things like that. Here, let me get you your drinks." A minute later, Alwin sat down, in the red chair, took a swallow of his nectar and stated, "There is no Gila lizard, and it was the only way I could alert Queen Diane to what is going on in this valley without being killed by those goons in the cave."

"And what is that?" questioned Thor.

"About 6 months ago, a blue fungus growing deep in one of the caves in the mountains on the north side of the valley was discovered. A one of our scientist mixed it with other chemicals and it increased its potency by two hundred percent. That fungus is now being mixed with an acid, crystallized then put in a sphere. All it takes to ignite that stuff is a small spark to explode it into a deadly cloud." Sam stared at Alwin and said, "Interesting story and how did you find out about this?"

"I have a perch on the north side of the valley where I sit, relax and I overheard a bunch of goons talking about it."

Thor asked, "Do you know where this cave is?"

"Sure do. It's in the shadow of that tall rock formation that juts two hundred feet above the forest canopy." Thor glanced at Pixy and asked, "Can you scoot out that cave and get back to me?"

"Consider it done Sir." and flew out the door.

CHAPTER 8

The Will-o'-the-wisp On the Attack

Alwin stared at Patrick, Gideon Bear, Sam and Thor and groaned, "You have got to be kidding me? No offense, but, how is a Leprechaun, a sprite, a stuffed bear, has been admiral, and a hero wannabe going to take down those professional killers? What I need is The Galaxy Sentinel, his sidekick, Admiral Sam the Stout, and Gideon the Avenger, I have been hearing so much about."

Thor chuckled as he stared at Sam and asked, "Shall we tell him? Or let him remain in the dark."

"Tell me what?" Alwin paused, stared at his company, and stated, "You don't mean to tell me, you are them."

"In the flesh, oh, Gideon is the Avenging Bear!"

Alwin stood to his feet, put his hand on his hips and said to Gideon, "Okay, Half Point. I have a lifelike manikin in my basement I use to scare away animals with. Show me what you can do."

In the dank dark cellar, Gideon sized up the six feet six dummy clad in ragged, black clothes, glanced up at Thor, as if to say, "Is this guy for real?"

Alwin laughed, "Just what I thought. You brought a child play thing to a fight. I don't know what you guys are trying to pull, but get out of my house, you bunch of phonies before I have you arrested for fraud."

Patrick hollered, "That's it Alwin! I've stood here and listened to your insults long enough! Apologize to me friends, or you are toast."

"What are you going to do, Imp, kick me in my shins?"

Patrick quickly rubbed his hands together and stretched them out in front of him. Sending a bolt of lightning from the tip of his fingers, hitting the wall on the other side of the basement, and then stated through clenched teeth, "That was a warning blast. Tell my friends you are sorry, or the next bolt will be right through you."

Alwin threw up his hand and shouted, "Alright, alright, alright! You're who you say you are. But, how are you going to take out The Dreaded 12?"

"Leave that up to us."

A loud crash caught everyone's attention. Thor muttered, "Pixy's hurt." quickly spun around and raced upstairs to find the sprite laying on the living room rug with several round burns to her back and legs. Patrick rushed to his wife's side rolled her on her back to see if she was still breathing. Pixy grimaced from the pain and reported, "It's worse than we thought, Sir. The entrance to the cave is heavily guarded, with 4 portable energy cannons strategically placed. The worst part is, they have set up an energy dampening field around the cave entrance. Meaning, they can shoot at us, but we can't shoot at them."

Thor touched his computer watch and said, "Cathy, I need 4 of those AK-47s we have in storage with the ammo, and my carbine rifle with the silencer. Then, have Tippy and Abbie meet me at my position as soon as they can. Sam and I have to exterminate a few vermin from the mountains around here."

"Understood, Sir. They should be at your position within the hour."

It wasn't long before, there was a knock at the back door. Alwin jumped up to see who it was and saw Tippy and Abbie standing on his back step and said, "Guys, there are two weird things just outside the back door. I think you'd better come and take a look."

Thor saw his two smiling daughters and said, "They're here to help. The tall one with the transparent wings, is Tippy. The younger one with the white fuzzy wings is Abbie and they are my two, adopted Will-o`-the-wisp daughters."

Abbie saw Pixy on the floor full of blood, threw open the door, rushed to her side, knelt, and cried.

Pixy clasped Abbie's hand and whispered, "I'll be alright. My Bug-a-Boo will make sure of that."

Tippy knelt by the injured sprite and remained silent for a minute. Then jerked her head up, stared Abbie in the eyes and stated, "It's time we called Prince Blue and ask him for a personal vendetta against those, cold hearted killers."

The two young Will-o'-the-wisps reached over Pixy, clasped hands, reared back, and let out a loud long bloodcurdling shriek that reverberated throughout the valley. Seconds later, a small black cloud appeared on the ceiling that grew ever larger with each passing second until it had reached the floor. Then a tall, deep blue, muscular male Will-o`-the-wisp, clad in gold apparel walked out. Abbie and Tippy sprang to their feet and bowed.

Prince Blue stared at Alwin and asked, "I am sorry for the intrusion, but when my subjects call I like to take care of the matter as quickly as possible." Blue turned to the two Wisps and asked, "What is your petition?"

Tippy spoke up and stated, "There is a group of savage killers loose in this valley. Abbie and I need your permission to do whatever it takes to stop them."

Blue turned his head, stared at Thor, and questioned, "Do you have anything to add to their statements?"

"Yes. A group called 'The 12' is holding the palace women scouts' hostage in the Dead Forest, to assure their reign of terror."

Prince Blue gazed at the two Wisps, let go a long guttural sound, spun around and vanished, in a flash of lighting."

Sam chuckled, "Blue is always the ham no matter what he does."

Thor ordered, "Abbie, take Pixy back to the Institute and meet us back here as fast as you can. Alwin pack some traveling food for us." Thor glanced at Tippy and questioned, "Where are the guns you were supposed to bring?"

"In the chicken-coop, for safe keeping."

Thor answered his computer watch and asked, "What can I do for you Rock?"

"The Blue Scarlet attacks have increased, Sir. There was an attack on the planet Kylee, two on Haskel Prime, and another attack on Avalon prime. Totaling eight hundred dead, with two hundred seriously injured in all."

"What about the gray spores?"

"They have a complex chemical compound that is making it difficult to reproduce. We have ten pounds ready to go but that's not going to be enough if the attacks keep increasing. How are things going at your end, Sir?"

"I'll inform you on that later, Thor out."

Abbie returned and stated, "Okaaay, I'm already to rip up a few humans."

Thor announced, "Get your gear packed, we leave at first light!"

Early the next morning, Thor was up before daybreak, walked outside and stared, at the mountains that rose up sharply on the north side of the valley. Then stared at the massive monolith at the base of the mountain that jutted high above the forest canopy.

Sam wandered out and asked, "Have a plan?"

"We send Tippy and Abbie in to take out the guards at the entrance to the cave."

"By the burns on Pixy, they knew she was coming long before she got there which means they have technology that we haven't even heard of yet."

"If I can get on top of that huge column of rocks jutting up I may be able to draw a bead on the guards."

"Remember, that's where Pixy was shot, and you're a bigger target."

"I'm aware of that Sam." Thor's eyes opened wide as he stared at his friend and stated, "There to types of scanning devices. Independent and series. The Independent scanners are great for picking up objects at close range. But, the series scanners are used to cover a wide area." Thor smiled and said, "But the series have one major flaw. You take out one, and the rest will follow."

"Like dominoes. But finding them is going to be the difficult part."

"Patrick may have a few tricks up his sleeve. It's time to wake everybody, we have work to do."Thor spotted a small air horn inside the chicken coop, picked it up, walked inside and let go a long blast. Abbie, who was sleeping on the couch tumbled on the floor, let go a scream, and then grumbled, "Nice way to give a body a heart attack."

"It's time to rise and shine."

"I'm rising but, I am not going to be Miss Sunshine."

The rest wandered out into the Livening room blurry eyes. Tippy moaned, "Who's the obnoxious one with the air-horn?"

"We leave in a half hour, so be ready or be left behind." Thor answered his computer watch and said, "What can I do for you, Cathy?"

"Tell Patrick Pixy isn't doing so well, and he should return as soon as possible."

"Okay, I'll tell him." Thor turned to the leprechaun and said, "Your wife has taken a turn for the worse."

"Thanks Boss, I'm on my way. Give those creeps one for me and Pixy." stated Patrick as he rushed out the door to his wife.

"Thor hollered, "Hold on there, Little Guy, you are not going anywhere until we pray for you and your wife."

After Patrick left, Thor turned to Sam and stated, "Now, it's personal."

Alwin stared at Thor's rifle and said, "That's an old Earth style1938 Carbine rifle customized with a large ammo clip and a scope, Niiiice."

"Thanks." stated Thor then shouted, "Okay everyone let's move out!"

Two hundred feet from the base of the mountain, by a tall Spruce Tree, Tippy pointed to a gray, baseball size sphere thirty feet in front of them and asked, "Do you want me to take it out?"

"Sure. Give it a try."

Tippy crept up to the sensory sphere, bent down to touch it, when a charge of energy from it jolted her hand. She grumbled, "Stupid thing bit me." then stated, "There's an energy field protecting the censer net."

"Step aside Tip, let's see what a chunk of lead will do to that thing." stated Thor and leveled his rifle at it.

Alwin muttered, "I don't think it is going to work."

Tippy glared at him and stated, "Keep your negative comments to yourself if you don't mind."

The bullet from Thor's rifle found its mark and shorted out the entire sensor network. Abbie looked at Tippy with a devilish grin and said, "Hey sis, you wanna give those guards by the cave something to worry about? What'd ya say we give them a sample of our famous screech?"

"Ready when you are sis. The two Will-o'-the-wisp reared back and let go a long nightmarish shriek that reverberated throughout the valley.

Alwin nervously glanced around and asked, "Would you ladies mind not doing that? It reminds me of a nightmare I had once."

"Kinda like Déjà-Vu?" Inquired Abbie.

"Ah, yeah. Something like that."

Abbie got in Alwin's face and said, "I know you. For a body that lives in an out of the way valley, you sure know a lot about things."

Thor whispered, "Look alive everybody, company's coming."

Everyone crouched behind bushes, boulders, and trees, poised and ready. Gideon scampered up a nearby tree and sat on a branch, with his katana in his paw.

Six renegades approached dressed in dark blue uniforms brandishing clear crystalline energy rifles. Alwin jumped up from behind a rock, waving his arms and shouting, "Don't shoot!"

One of the renegades leveled his energy rifle at Alwin and stated, "No one from the valley is allowed up here." a blast of blue light shout out of his gun, slammed into Alwin's arm cutting it off. Thor hollered, "Let them have it!"

The renegades quickly knelt, in a semicircle and lit up the woods with blue energy cutting through rocks and trees as a hail of lead struck their protective shield. Thor waved his rifle and hollered,

"We surrender!" Then slowly stood on his feet. Then motioned for the others to do the same.

The leader of the group of renegades, ordered, "Drop your weapons and stand over there by that fallen tree with your hands in the air. Okay men it is safe to turn off your personal shields they're not going to do anything now."

Sam smiled and said, "Never judge a book by its cover, or get cocky just because you think you have the upper hand."

"And what is that supposed to mean?" grumbled a renegade.

"Now, Gideon!" shouted Thor.

The bear sliced his blade horizontally as he jumped on top of the leader burying his katana in his neck. Tippy and Abbie's wings buzzed as they shot forward with a hair-raising shriek, tearing at their flesh. Abbie pointed to a renegade crouching behind a large gray rock. Tippy leaped on top of it and waved down at him. He pleaded, "Please don't kill me."

Tippy jumped down, picked him up by his throat and asked, "Why should I let you live? You and your cohorts have been brutally slaughtering over a thousand innocent men, woman, and children. Have you ever heard the horrifying screams from the people that stuff unleashed on them? Have you?"

The renegade whimpered, "No."

"Well I have." stated Tippy as she let the man drop to the ground. The man stood up and smirked, "Weakling."

Tippy clenched her fist, her eyes blazed with anger, as she glared at him, then slammed her fist on top of his head with such force that it drove his skull down inside his chest. Tippy watched the lifeless body fall to the ground, turned, and quietly walked away in silence.

Thor walked up to his daughter and inquired, "Are you gonna be alright?"

"Give me a minute or two."

CHAPTER 9

The Tomb

The group stood by the huge rock formation that jutted high above the forest canopy. Thor stated, "The cave should be about a hundred yards above the tree line. I can take out the two guards, at the cave entrance let's just pray they don't have an energy field blocking the entrance." Thor leaned against a tree, drew a bead on the guards and was ready to pull the trigger when Tippy placed her hand on her father's shoulder and said, "Please dad, no more killing. Let me handle this." Tippy approached her sister and said, "Are you ready to play the wounded duck routine?"

Abbie and Tippy opened the top five buttons on their jumpsuits, Abbie said, "I'll take the cute one the left, you take the ugly one on the right with the face fungus."

Remember, we're weak helpless female Wisps who have lost their way. Dad, Sam, when Abbie and I bring the men into the forest, you two take care of them."

The two sprites landed on the rocky sloops of the mountain, twenty feet from the guards, walked up to them. Tippy smiled and stated, "Hi, this is my friend Abbie and I'm Tippy, the boss sent us up here to put some pleasure into your guard duty. Tippy glanced at her sister rubbing her chest hoping to get his attention. Instead they leveled their energy rifles at them and fired sending Abbie and Tippy stumbling back 5 feet. Abbie glanced down at the large burned hole in the top half of her jumpsuit and grumbled, "I do not like men who burn the clothes off lady Wisps."

The guards fired again, striking the girls in the center of their chests leaving large holes in the upper half of their jumpsuit. Tippy politely muttered, "Don't you know you can't hurt a Will-o'-the- wisp with those toy guns. Now that you perverts have had a free peek my bare chest, how about if we give you a free flying lesson?"Tippy seized the guard by his shirt, let go a screech and hurled him over her head and into the trees below. Abbie was busy trying to cover her bare chest and was thrown to the ground by the guard and rammed the barrel of his rifle in her mouth and said, "Let's see it you can shake this off."

Seeing her sister in trouble, Tippy walked up behind the man, took a deep breath, and let out a lone ultra-high screech. The guard screamed, as he dropped his rifle, grabbed his ears, and then collapsed on the rocks dead.

Tippy helped Abbie to her feet and asked, "Are you alright?"

"Yeah, Sorry I got embarrassed when my boobs were exposed to that creep."

Tippy squatted behind a boulder with Abbie and hollered, "Hey Dad! Can you bring our backpacks up to us? Abbie and I have a wardrobe malfunction!"

Once the girls were decent, Thor and Sam examined the cave entrance, Sam shook his head and stated, "Without the proper scanning equipment to find out what this energy barrier's frequency is that's blocking the cave entrance. There is no way we will be able to get in."

Patrick walked out from behind a large rock and said, "Top o` the morning to you me lads."

"And the rest of the day to yourself," answered Thor, "What are you doing back here, when you're supposed to be with your wife."

Patrick looked down and said, "There's not a whole lot I can do there but, sit and wait. Patrick glanced at the cave entrance and said, "Laddies and lassies, stand back this is gonna be a big blast." Patrick quickly rubbed his hands together for a good thirty seconds before stretching them out in front of him, letting go a charge of lightning from his fingers that slammed into the energy barrier. When he saw, the shield turns red, he hollered, "Run for cover! She's gonna blow!"

A tremendous explosion shook the ground side showering the mountainside with rocks.

Thor stood in the cave entrance and stared at the tunnel shaped like an elongated oval laying on its side that disappeared into the darkness and stated, "Sam any signs of that dampening field Still on?"

"Nope, nada, I did a scan of the cave but found nothing."

"What about that blue fungi? Is that in this cave?"

"I am picking up something, but, can't tell what it is."

Thor bellowed, "Okay, let's move out! Sam, you take point, Tippy you bring up the rear."

Abbie stared at her sister and snickered.

Tippy grumbled, "Don't even say it."

Five hundred feet in the cave, Sam stated, "Watch your step because it's all downhill from here."

A half hour later they came to a huge rock wall with a horizontal slit just big enough for them to crawl through. Thor asked, "Patrick crawl in there and see what's on the other side."

Five minutes later, Patrick shouted, "Come on through!"

After Thor, Gideon and Abbie went through, Sam stared at the opening, patted his stomach, and said, "No way am I going to fit in there I am too round in the belly."

"You can do it Sir," stated Tippy behind Sam.

"Okay but if I get stuck I'm gonna blame you. Sam crawled part way in then stated, "That's it I can't go any further."

Tippy crept up behind Sam, laid flat on her stomach, took hold of the bottom of Sam's shoes, and asked, "Can you suck it in just a tad more?"

"I'll try. What's your plan?"

"I have just enough room to use my wings." Tippy's groaned as her wings buzzed pushing Sam through inch by inch. Thor stared in the crevice and inquired, "Everything okay in there?"

"We're inching along." replied Sam, trying to keep a positive attitude about the whole situation. Suddenly, Sam and Tippy shot out of the fissure, as if they were shot out of a cannon. Sam hit the ground, rolled several times, stood up and stated, "I am not going to do that again."

Patrick flashed his light around the immense cavern, walked to a control panel by the fissure and said, "You won't have to," then threw a switch. The horizontal fissure slowly opened. Patrick sat on a boulder and said, "If it weren't for this rock coming loose we would never gotten through."

Tippy picked up a boulder some six feet in diameter, rolled it to where Patrick sat and said, "No offense Sam, but I'm jamming this thing open with a bigger rock."

Patrick hit another switch that turned on the light. Thor stared down into a huge hole and said, "Looks like the only way is down. Tip, you wanna fly down and see if there is another way?"

Tippy grabbed a flashlight and flew down into the dark hole. A minute later, metal steps slid out from the side of the hole creating a circular staircase down to the bottom.

In the hole, Tippy directed everyone to a smooth, round tunnel that lead into a vast cavern. Thor knelt down and touched flat slimy blue fungus growing on a rock, then flashed his light around the cavern and said, "This is definitely where the fungus grew, but it looks like somebody cleaned the place out of the fungi." Suddenly a small explosion sent rocks down, blocking the only way out.

Patrick hollered, "We're trapped!"

"No, I don't think so. There has to be another way out." stated Thor.

"What makes you say that, Boss?"

"The controls to the rock wall, and the stairs are on the inside, so there has to be a back door to this cavern somewhere."

Sam inquired, "Thor. Shall we set it up now?"

"No time like the present."

Sam put his backpack down and said, "A little light over here if you please." Sam took out several long silver rods, fastened a stand with a 1 by 2-foot frame on a swivel. He then stretched a clear piece of plastic over the frame.

Tippy asked, "What's that for?"

"You have heard of night-vision goggles. This is a night vision lens, plus it will let me know if there is a hidden passageway in here. So, relax while Thor and I check this cavern out."

Sam touched a small button on the right side of the frame and the transparent plastic sheet turned a transparent blue.

After an hour of searching the cavern with the night vision lens, Sam spotted something on the far wall and asked, "Abbie. Can you walk to the wall opposite where we came in? There is something there, but I can't make it out."

"You're right, Sam, there is something here, but I can't budge it."

Patrick approached Abbie, took out a marker, placed an X on the wall and said, "Stand back," Then rubbed his hands together and stretched them out in front of him. A powerful charge of electricity leaped off his finger tips and slammed into the wall pulverizing the rock. Thor sat down and leaned back against a stalagmite and stated, "Where to from here? I don't know. I was hoping we could stop those cold-hearted murderers by cutting off their supply of blue accelerate, but it seems they are always two steps ahead of us at every turn we make." He then fell asleep.

Sam sat on Thor's right and said, "You're right Thor we're just chasing our tails; we might as well give up on this case. Sam closed his eyes and drifted off to sleep. Abbie was stretched out on a rock next to Patrick. Tippy muttered, "Gotta go for help." took a dozen steps and collapsed on some rocks.

Gideon being a Three-Dimensional Particle Acceleration Bear, wasn't affected by the noxious gas. He waddled to Thor's right wrist, tapped his computer watch and contacted Cherry. When a three-dimensional image of her head appeared above the watch the bear frantically waved his paws trying to tell Cherry that something was wrong. Cherry stared at the bear and asked, "Is there something wrong Squirt?"

Gideon raised Thor's arm and showed his face to Cherry. She quickly replied, "Hold on, I'll contact the Institute right away."

Thor opened his eyes in the Institute's infirmary sometime later, with Doctor Chrissy staring him in the face and he stated, "Good Lord Chrissy, you look like crap. There is a remedy for your condition you know, it's called sleep. You should try it. It'll do wonders for you."

"Don't get smart with me Mister. I don't know what you 4 got yourselves into but it took me 5 days trying every remedy I knew just to keep you guys alive. By the way, how's your head?"

Thor closed his eyes saying, "It hurts at the slightest sound, so do me a favor and whisper."

"Good, the drug is working. You are going to stay in bed until I say so."

"I don't care how my head huts, I can't stay here because I have work to do." As soon as Thor sat up the room begin to spin. Chrissy hollered, "I need a barf bucket in Thor's room ASAP!"

Cherry rushed to her husband's side with a red plastic bucket and said, "I am glad you are a wake. Now lay back down and the room will stop spinning."

"Clever idea. How are the others?"

"Just like you. Now, lie down. Just to let you know, you four have been out for five days."

"Chrissy told me that. What about the palace scouts that were captured in the Dead Forest? Someone has to go after them."

"Thor. Do I have to put a piece of tape over your mouth to keep you quiet?"

"No. What about Pixy? How is she doing?"

"I'm warning you Thor. One more word and I I'm getting the tape."

A week later, Thor dragged himself into his office, sat behind his desk; put his head in his hands moaning, "I never knew a person could feel this lousy."

Lacy opened the office door, stuck her head in and asked, "Sir. Do you want me to get you a cup of coffee?"

"Yes, please."

Gideon waddled in a few minutes later with a mug of coffee in his paws and let go a squeak.

Thor took the mug from the bear and said, "Hey squirt. I see Cathy gave you a mouth. Oh, thanks for saving us back in the cave. I owe you one big time."

Gideon handed Thor a note that read, Moonbeam needs to see you at the tram tunnel right away.

Later, Moonbeam met Thor at the tram dig and asked, "What do you think?"

Thor stared at the wooden structure with its thatched roof, and its bamboo sides and said, "Impressive."

An excited Moonbeam shouted, "Just wait until you see the inside, Sir."

Inside, Thor studied the tropical trees, birds and commented, "You have outdone yourself. But what about the tram tunnel? How is that coming along?"

"The tunnel is almost to the beach; the elevator and emergency staircase are finished. The tram station will be finished in two days."

"Keep up the decent work."

Sam approached Thor and said, "We have to get to the forest right away. Things are heating up."

CHAPTER 10

The Woman in The Water

Tom, a tall man with red hair, in his late twenties entered Thor's office with his wife Susie, a short perky woman in her mid-twenties. Thor inquired, "What can I do for you two?"

Tom spoke up, "As you know my wife Susie and I teach Sunday School at the Christ Tabernacle on Avalon Prime and I preach. When you return to the Agatharchides Valley, my wife and I would like to go with you."

"And your reason for leaving the Institute is?"

"I want to start a church there."

Thor smiled and asked, "What will you be teaching the people there?"

"Salvation, healing, deliverance, whatever the believer needs it, has been provided through the Cross of Christ. I will not preach any twelve-step program is not gospel but dead religion."

"You convinced me, so pack your things because Sam and I leave within the hour. Oh, I will also sport your minister in the Agatharchides Valley. Also, while you two are there, I need you to be my eyes and ears."

"Consider it done, Sir."

"When we get there, I will introduce you to Nina and her husband Virge, a couple who live in the valley and I know, they will be a great help in getting you two started."

Back in Agatharchides Valley, Thor, Cherry, Sam, Tom and his wife were walking across the stone bridge. Thor stated, "Nina and Virge live on the other side of the valley. Cherry turned her head and asked, "Thor, Hon, is that a second sun up there in the west?"

"It could be a sun-dog." Thor stared at the phenomenon, when a star cruiser roared out of the clouds and descended to one hundred feet above the ground. Sam hollered, "Hit the dirt!"

Thor looked at the huge craft as it scrapped the tops of houses, slamming into the mountain at the far eastern end of the valley. He touched his computer watch and stated, "Dave, tell the Queen, a star cruiser just crashed in the Agatharchides Valley."

A huge blue cloud rose from the rubble of the ship and drifted towards town. Thor reported over his computer watch, "There may not be anyone left in the valley because a Blue Scarlet cloud is coming out of the wreckage and heading this way. Thor out."

The people of the valley first stared at the strange sight, then a warning bell began to sound, telling everybody to head for the safety of mountains.

Cherry pointed to a crowd swiftly approaching and said, "It's time we make tracks before we are tramp on!"

High on the side of the west side of the mountain, Cherry's heart sank as she watched in horror as countless number of people that were caught by the caustic blue cloud, filling the valley with agonizing scream of people being dissolved by the caustic cloud.

Suddenly, 6 aircraft swooped down, sprayed the cloud of blue death with gray spores, turning the cloud into a swirling mass harmless of blue and scarlet. Tom turned to his wife and said, "Looks like we came at the right time."

Thor spotted Nina and Virge in the crowd of people returning and caught their attention. They gave Thor and Cherry a warm welcome and Thor introduced Tom and Susie and said, "That they want to start a church here in the valley."

"Excellent," stated Virge, "You can stay with us, until you get settled."

Tom stared at the black smoke rising from the wreckage and said, "First thing we do is see if there are any survivors in the wreckage and asked, "Virge, can you organize a rescue party?"

Cherry turned to her husband and said, "I'm gonna stay here, and take care of the ones who were injured by the cloud."

Thor kissed his wife and said, "Help from the Queen should be arriving soon. Sam and I have to head southeast and see if we can rescue those women from the Dead Forest."

Hours later, Thor and Sam left the woods, Sam glanced at his watch and stated, "What do you say we stay by that pond over there for the night?"

"Sounds good. You want two try your skill at Fishing?"

At the pond, Sam spotted a woman's clothes spread on a nearby bush and a yellow blanket on the grass with a tube of sunscreen lotion, a thermos full of coffee, and a romance novel next to a woman's pocketbook. Thor stated, "She has to be around here somewhere. Sam, you look in the bushes, I'll check the pond."

A few minutes later, Thor hollered, "I found her! She's over here by the bank! With a small dart in her thigh."

Thor picked up the woman and wrapped her in the blanket, Sam stated, "I found her address. She lived a half mile north of here."

Spotting a lovely white cottage surrounded with tall blue flowers, with tall cedar trees here and there. Sam opened the blue door, and Thor put the woman on the bed in her room. Picked up a King James Bible on her nightstand, opened it and found a note when she dedicated her life to Christ. Thor tapped his computer watch and said, "Get me Patrick."

The leprechaun walked up behind him with his wife Pixy and said, "You called Boss?"

"Yes, Sam and I found an unconscious young woman in the pond not too far from here with this dart in her tushy. I put her in on the bed, see what you can do to help her."

Sam stated, "I am going to see what she has to eat, I am starved."

Thor heard a noise coming from outside, parted the curtain in the liven room and saw six men standing twenty feet from the house. Sam walked up to Thor munching on a sandwich and asked, "What's up?"

"It looks like we have company and by the way my watch is buzzing their all renegades disguised as humans."

Sam handed Thor a Winchester rifle he found and said, "You might want to take this along. I already took the liberty of loading it."

One of the six bellowed, "Galaxy Sentinel! You have just five minutes to come out, or we'll come in after you!"

Pixy approached Thor with her head down and said, "There was nothing Patrick could do for her. The poison that was injected in her system from the dart was too powerful."

"Is she awake?"

"Yes."

Thor walked in the bedroom, sat on the bed next to the woman, held her hand and vowed, "Ma'am. Trust me when I say the people who did this to you will pay."

With a smile on her face the woman whispered, "My name is Katie. Why did those men try to kill me?"

"I don't know. But I am about to find out."

Thor walked outside with his Winchester in his right hand and asked, "What is it you want?"

"Now that we have the undivided attention of the Alliance. There are some demands that has to be met or thousands more will die."

"Don't you mean, slaughtered?"

"The Institute that is hidden in the Asteroid Belt 'The Rock Pile' will be destroyed. You are to surrender to the 12 and your workers are to be handed over for punishment."

Thor leveled his rifle at them and stated, "Don't hold your breath."

"You who has none violence ethics code is threatening us? I don't think so." the six men slowly walked towards Thor with their weapons pointing at him.

Thor warned, "One more step and I'll fire."

They kept coming, Thor dropped to the ground and fired six shots. Sprang to his feet, spun to his right, and peppered the trees with bullets. Sam and Patrick rushed out of the house, ducked down by the flowers and fired on Thor's left side killing several more men. Upon hearing a scream coming from the house they rushed inside to find Pixy in the bedroom trying to protect the woman from four renegades. Thor warned, "Pixy. Don't shoot or you will hit Kate."

Pixy stated firmly, "Gentleman. Turn yourselves around and leave before you are dog meat."

One man stated in disgust, "You're only 38 inches tall. What can you do to us? Get out of the way so we can finish what we started."

Pixy reared back and let go a screech sounding more like an animal than a sprite. Morphed into a tall, seven-foot red Will-o-the-wipes, grabbed one renegade by his throat and drove her fist through his chest, slammed him on the floor. Let go another screech and ripped into the other two men tearing them to pieces. Pixy approached the last one cowering on the floor picked him up by his throat and asked, "Thor, do you have a message for him to take back to his boss?"

"I've got him Pixy." She morphed back into a normal sprite as Thor warned, "Tell your boss, that I am coming for him. Now get out of here!"

Thor turned to Sam and asked, "Help me gather up the dead renegades so I can send them back to Montros.

Patrick put his arm around his wife and asked, "Are you going to be alright me Fire-Fly?"

With a tear in her eye, Pixy stated "Give me a few minutes. I hate having to kill but letting them continue slaughtering countless thousands of innocent men, women and children would be a crime against humanity."

Katie sat up in bed and said, "Come here Pixy. I think you need a hug."

Patrick gazed at Kate and stated, "You're not supposed to be sitting up Lassie."

"Why not? I feel great."

"You're supposed to be dying from the poison on the dart you were shot with."

Katie smiled and said, "I guess the Lord is not finished with me yet. Now will you guys kindly leave my bedroom, so a lady can get dressed?"

Katie walked into the livening room dressed in a lovely pink blouse and yellow skirt and asked, "What would everyone like to eat? Better yet, let me surprise you all."

After the meal, Thor handed Katie the Winchester and said, "Thank you for the use of the gun."

"You can have that thing. Somebody gave it to me several months ago, and

I didn't have a clue as to what it was used for. Oh a, Sir. Could you have everyone gather in the den for coffee, and chocolate cake?"

Katie served everyone then inquired, "Why are you all here? Mind you, I am grateful for the help and you all being here but the last time anyone visited me was a year ago."

Thor spoke up, "My friend Sam and I were on our way to the Dead Forest to rescue the palace women scouts when Sam and I found you in the pond not too far from here."

Katie blushed and said, "I go there once a week, with a good book, a lunch and go swimming. I own the land, and no one has ever bothered me there because my house is the only house around for 7 miles in all directions." Katie paused for a moment, turned to Thor and inquired, "My mind is a little foggy about what happened. Would you mind telling me where you found me?"

Thor smiled and replied, "Your swimsuit was by the edge of the pond ma'am and was shot by a dart when you were swimming. We located your home, brought you here and put you in your bed."

Katie grew flustered and asked, "I do not swim, and do I dear ask what you gents did to me after you put me in my bed?"

Sam quickly answered, "You were covered over right after Thor put you in bed, then he immediately called Patrick and his wife Pixy to try and help you. And no, we did not take advantage of you while you were unconscious. I am married to a lovely woman and so is Thor."

"That's a relief, you guys had me worried for a moment. Did you say you were going to the Dead Forest? Because without a map, you'll be wandering around for months before you actually find it."

"I assume you have one." stated Thor.

Katie stated with a smile, "That's right. I have the only map left. All the other maps showing that area disappeared 6 months ago"

Thor stood to his feet and said, "I am the Galaxy Sentinel and run a complex that has 250 people all starving for a place to go for a picnic. Would you mind it if some of the families from the Institute use your land for a getaway?"

Tears ran down Katie's face as she stated, "They are welcome to come here anytime they want, because I own two hundred acres of land all dying to be used."

"You do know you are going to be swamped with woman adoring your beautiful gardens around your home."

"It will be a welcome change from the isolated life I've been living." Katie glanced at the clock on the wall and said, "There are several spare bedrooms upstairs you are more than welcome to stay for the night."

"Sounds good," stated Thor.

Pixy quickly stated, "I'll take first watch!"

CHAPTER 11

The Dead Forest

Katie was up early the next day and had the morning meal on the table before everyone was up. Pixy sat next to her husband at the table, gave him a peck on the cheek saying, "I'm gonna stay here with Katie just in case more of those thugs come snooping around."

After the morning meal, Thor placed the map on the kitchen table. He then asked Katie, "Where are we on this map?"

Katie pointed to a small blue spot in the center of the map and said, "That's the pond where you found me, my house is just north of there. The Dead Forest is a good day's walk west of here. When you see the Green Mountain range, look for a large gap between the mountains that will be the entrance to the Black Forest."

Thor rose to his feet saying, "Ready Sparky? Come on Sam we have some women to rescue."

Three o'clock that afternoon Thor, Patrick, and Sam entered a clearing, Thor paused and stared the mountains in the distance and said, "I'd say we have another day to go before get there. What do you say we camp here for the night?"

Patrick sat down took off his shoes and moaned, "Good, me dogs are barking something fierce."

Thor made a campfire, Sam gazed at the leprechaun and inquired, "Patrick, what did you find on Katie when you examined her?"

"There were a few pale red round marks all over her body. She is probably allergic to the poison she was shot with. Why do you ask?"

I believe Miss Katie that she doesn't swims. I think the 12 are behind the Blue Scarlet. The men that attacked Kate's house must have found her swimming, tortured her, then shot her with a poison dart."

"For what purpose?"

"Are you sure Katie was shot with a dart with deadly poison on it?"

"Yeah. Why?"

"Do you still have the dart with you?"

"Sure do." Patrick took out his medical scanner and checked the dart Katie was shot with and said, "This is weird. There is not even a trace of poison on the dart."

"With all that has happened up until now including what happened to Katie can you generalize what her attacker plans might be?"

"I'd say they tortured Katie then made it look like she was she was short with a poison dart while skinny-dipping, then used the sap from the Red Snow Orchid found only on Avalon Prime to make it look like she was dying. The side effect from that sap leaves the person mind thirsty for suggestion. They then told Kate to give us the map to the Dead Forest."

"But why did they go through all that elaborate scam? When they could have just shot her with the dart." questioned Sam.

Thor stated, "Montronians love theatrics, that's why." Thor tossed the map to Sam and said they used Katie to get our attention, so she could give us the map that has been sprayed with a tracking compound, and the Twelve could track of us once we reached the Dead Forest."

"Do you think Katie is working for the 12?"

"No. she was just a pawn they used to get our attention. But I have a plan to throw them off track. Sam hand me your energy pistol if you please."

"Here, what do you have in mind?"

"I have had my eye on a white-tailed deer grazing several hundred feet behind you. No one move."Thor stunned the dear tied the map to its neck then chased it south of their position. Thor sat back down made a pot of coffee, slowly reached for his Winchester with his right hand saying, "We are not out of the woods yet. Sam, you see those trees on the edge of this meadow? Up in that huge maple I think there is a sniper."

Patrick smiled devilishly and said, "Let me take care of him Boss." Patrick slowly stood to his feet, quickly rubbed his hands together then stretched them out in front of him sending a bolt of electricity across the field splintering the tree into thousands of pieces.

Sam suggested, "Shall we go see what we got?"

Thor walked up to the man lying on the ground smoldering from Patrick's blast and said, "Renegade, when is your boss gonna learn that he is not gonna win. You're out of here." Thor pointed his ruby pen at him and sent him back to Montros for punishment.

Back at camp, Sam took a swallow of his coffee and questioned, "Do you think they will eventually stop trying to kill us?"

"Yeah. When they are all dead. But not before."

Sam inquired, "Do you think we should set a watch tonight?"

"Set your scanner to sound an alarm, then put it on a wide loop. That should take care of anyone trying to come in the camp."

Unable to sleep Thor lay quietly in the dark listening to the night creatures when his sensitive hearing picked up footsteps approaching the camp. Thor sprang to his feet, tackled the individual and caught the fragrance of familiar perfume and asked, "Cherry, is that you?"

"Nice to see you too sweetheart."

Thor helped his wife to her fee, gave her a hug and asked, "What are you doing here?"

"Queen Diane just received a message from the 12 that said if you come any closer to the Dead Forest, they will kill the women."

"Well, it looks like we go home then. Patrick in the morning have Pixy bring Katie to the Institute. Cherry, you, Sam, and I are going to see the Queen, I have a trump card I want to play. But first, we get some sleep."

Back at the castle the next day, Cherry went to her room and Thor approached Diane and asked, "I need a sample of DNA from all the women scouts. Once I have that we must go back home. Because there is nothing more I we can do here."

"Aren't you going to rescue the woman?" inquired Queen Diane.

"They will kill those women if anyone even things about getting close. But I have an idea that I think will work."

Thor walked in his room and hollered, "Cherry! Where are you?"

"In the bathroom."

Thor entered the bathroom, saw his wife soaking in a tub of turquoise translucent goo, smiled and asked, "What did you do? Fall asleep already?"

"I was so anxious to try this stuff when we got back that I think I put just a tad too much in. Now I seem to be stuck."

Thor picked up the package, read the directions and said, "This stuff has to be kept at a constant ninety-eight degrees or it will turn into a solid."

"Thor! Stop fooling around and get me out of this!"

"Be back in a bit, I'll get the guards to help me get you out." and left.

Cherry screamed, "Thor! Don't you dear do that! Do you hear me? I don't want those guys to see my butt! Get back in here this minute!"

Thor poked his head in the bathroom and said, "Just kidding. The heat from your body might have kept the goo soft around you so I should be able to pull you out." Thor reached behind Cherry, slipped his arms under her shoulders, and pulled. A minute later Cherry was free from her soft prison.

Thor suggested, "Why don't you step in the shower and wash the rest of that goo off you." and tweaked her butt. Later, Cherry crawled in bed and was fast asleep in seconds.

Back at the Institute a day later, Thor examined the new elevator cross the hall from his office that maintenance was putting the finishing touches on and asked, "What Pray tell is this for?"

"It's the elevator to the underground tram station. Thanks Sir for having it built."

Thor entered his office and asked his secretary, "Lacy, find Moonbeam and have her report to my office, immediately!"

Moonbeam joyfully bounced in Thor's office all smiles proud of her accomplishment and asked, "You wanted to see me, Sir?"

"I thought I gave you the okay to build an underground tram to the beach. Why did you build it to the Institute instead?"

"I did. There's one going to the beach too."

Trying to keep his temper, Thor stated, "Let me get this straight. You took it upon yourself to dig a tram tunnel to the Institute and the beach."

Moonbeam smiled sheepishly and stated, "I also built one to the beach from The Institute." Moonbeam then quickly added, "The tram will come in handy during the rainy season."

"Do you have power backup encase of an emergency?"

"Oh, yes Sir. There is a backup generator in case of power failure. Plus, if all else fails the back end of the tram opens so the passengers can walk back to the station."

"I see you have thought of everything. Good. But, next time consult me before you make any changes to any future projects."

"Yes Sir!"

"One last question. How many tub trams did you dig?"

"Six Sir two from the housing project to the beach two from the beach to the Institute and two from the Institute to the housing project. Because there must be a tram going and coming. Oh, all the underground tram stations are prefab building."

Thor silently stared at Moonbeam for several seconds then inquired, "What about the sprites Constance, Darlene, and Susanna?"

"Do you want to know?"

"Yes, I want to know! What are they up to?"

"Mimi is doing great. But, Constance, Darlene and Susanna are still at it no matter what I threaten them with. They put a fake snake in the hot springs when Missy and her lady sprite friends were soaking their sore bodies after a long day. Then they sprayed a chemical on Cathy so when she went in the water she turned red. Lastly, they gave Misty some sleeping medicine, then put her on the beach in the buff. Fortunately, it was in the afternoon on a work day and only a few guys saw her naked. But poor Misty looks like a lobster because of her sunburn."

"Where is Missy now?"

"In the infirmary."

Thor walked in the infirmary and asked, "Chrissy, is it alright if I talk to Misty?"

"Sure, go ahead."

Thor approached the sprites bed, saw the redness of her skin, and asked, "Does it hurt much?"

"The doctor gave me something to cool the burning but I think I will visit my fire Pixie friend for a few months."

"Embarrass because a few guys saw you on the beach, nude?"

"You know it, Sir."

Moonbeam walked up to Thor in the infirmary and stated, "I think I have a way to fix those mischievous Sprites once and for all."

Patrick rushed in the infirmary all out of breath and stated, "There's been a Blue Scarlet attack at the natural water slide! There are at least a dozen staff members down."

"How did it happen?" inquired Thor.

"Some of the married couples were having a get together at the water slide today when the blue cloud appeared as they slid down the slide eat the skin off their bodies."

Chrissy hit the emergency alarm and announced, "This is a medical emergency! All available personal is to report to the water slide!"

"Moonbeam stated, "We can take the Tram it's faster."

Cherry, her clone Cherish, and Rose rushed in the infirmary and asked, "Tell what to do Doc?"

"I need you to setup a triage on the beach before the wounded are transferred to the underground beach Tram Depot. There is an herb solution in the stainless-steel tubs in the corner of my office. Soak some bed sheets in it, wring them out and bring them down to the beach Tram Station and wrap the victims in the sheets. That will help them until I can take care of them."

Cherry inquired, "How is a cold wet sheet going to help when they'll be in shock?"

"The body heat will cause a thermal reaction in the herbs sheet-soaked solution. Plus, the herbs will help ease their pain."

Chrissy handed Thor a sprayer and said, "When we get here, put this on and wash down each victim before they're put on the stretcher."

Thor, and Chrissy rushed to the elevator with Moonbeam caring several boxes of gauze bandages. As soon as the elevator door opened on the beach tram station, Moonbeam charged to a long clear crystalline capsule some 12 feet long and 5 feet high and hollered, "Get in, get in I'll handle the controls!"

The tram slipped silently through the round tunnel and was at its destination in m minutes. Moonbeam jumped out of the tram, after Thor and Chrissy, pushed a button that flattened the seats and stated, "With the hooks on the inside, we can fit 2 stretchers in the tram. Oh, the elevator to the beach is just on the other side of the depot."

On the beach, Thor's heart sank saw his staff writhing in pain stripped of their skin by the Blue Scarlet cloud. He took out his energy pistol, put it on wide dispersal and stunned them.

At that time women from the Institute began to show up by the way of retrieval computer wanting to help. Thor instructed, "You, grab a male staff member, bring a victim into the beach house, hose them down with this, then put them on a stretcher and send them to Cherry at the Beach Depot who will wrap them in the herb soaked sheet. Ladies, you do the same to the women."

Just then a tall renegade appeared twenty set from Thor holding a blue sphere in his hands and said, "I am glad you all are here. I can take care of all of you right now."

Thor questioned, "What, you're not gonna blow up some innocent people, or use a replica"

"The Boss wants me to record your suffering as the flesh slowly dissolves off your bones."

Moonbeam picked up a rock and hollered, "Crawl back under that rock you came from!" And threw it hitting the sphere releasing the toxic gas. The renegade fell to the sand writhing and screaming in agony. As Thor hollered 1, "Everyone get back!"

Once the caustic cloud had dissipated, Thor stared at the remains, touched his computer watch and said, "Security, erect the magnetic shield around the planetoid and rotate the shield harmonic vibrations every 15 minutes Thor, out."

Thor picked up a metallic disk some 2 inches in diameter from the renegades remains then asked, "Moonbeam, do you have a piece of paper and pencil? I'd like to send a message those Twelve."

Thor wrote, to the 12, your days are numbered. The Galaxy Sentinel. He placed the note on the remains, put the. Disk on top of that and activated it sending the renegade's remains back to where he came from.

Moonbeam look up at Thor and asked, "Are you still up for dealing with those she-devils? Because they're over there by the beach house talking."

Thor walked up to the mischievous sprites, clan in their skimpy bathing suits, glared down them and asked, "I need three people to manage the tram stations are you ladies up for the task?"

Constance quickly replied, "Sure just tell us when to report to work."

"Constance, you take the Beach Depot, Darlene, you take Institute Depot, and Susanna, you take the Housing Project Depot. Now, you guys are sure you can handle the job? Because it's a lot of responsibility."

"No problem." reply Constants.

"Good. Because you three start your new jobs in ten minutes. Oh, and just remember, one mess up and you will have to give an account for the lives that were injured."

After the sprites rushed off to their jobs, Moonbeam bellowed, "Are you nuts? That's the last thing those three Losers need, is responsibility."

"Responsibility may be just the thing to straighten them out. A good swift kick in the pants didn't work. Playfully this will."

CHAPTER 12

Undercover

Thor sat at his desk the next morning, called the Chief of police on the planet Kylee and said, "I am turning over the investigation of the scientist Mr. Tatsuya."

"What for?"

"Mr. Tatsuya and the Hummer-gene were working together to build a super energy cannon that will destroy a target anywhere in the galaxy from a specific location. The Hummer-gene killed his granddaughter, but I am not sure how Mr. Tatsuya fits in the murder and I don't have the time to investigate it further."

"When can I expect the file on Mr. Tatsuya?"

"In a day or two."

Lacy stated over the intercom, "The DNA for those women scouts just arrived Sir."

Thor tapped his intercom and said, "Will Cathy please come to my office." Just then Sprite Missy walked in Thor's office and said, "Cathy will be here in a few minutes Sir."

"What in the world are you eating that smells funny?"

"It's a marshmallow fluff, sardine and peanut butter sandwich. You want me to make you one?"

"Ahhh, no thanks. While you are here. I need to speak to you about the sprite menu."

"Did someone barf because I served Sheppard's pie one day last week?"

"No. It was a big hit. Do you think you can serve it again tomorrow?"

"Sure can."

Thor put Missy in a head lock and briskly rubbed his knuckles across the top of her head with Missy hollering, "Not the Noogies! I just had my hair done!"

Cherry entered the office, looked at Missy with her hair standing up and inquired, "Did you just stick your finger in a light socket?"

Missy promptly stormed out the door with a scowl on her face as Cherry questioned her husband, "Are you teasing poor Missy again?"

Cathy walked in the office and inquired, "You wanted to see me Sir?"

"Yes. I have the DNA from the palace's women scouts. I want you to do a scan on the moon of the Dark planet for them."

"And if they're not there? Then what Sir?"

"Then you scan every planet in the Alliance until you have found them."

Thor turned to Cherry and asked, "Are you ready? There is a waiter on the planet Avalon Prime that needs looking into."

"A waiter? You have got to be kidding. A waiter? I would not miss this for all the gold in the Galaxy."

Thor appeared in small town on the planet of Avalon Prime, in a flash of pale blue light, turned to his wife and asked, "Seeing that it's still early, why don't we grab a cup of coffee?"

Sitting at the counter in 'The Full Cup' Cafe, Cherry took a swallow of her Hazelnut coffee, stared at the waiter, and inquired, "Is that you Guy?"

"Cherry, I haven't seen you since we were in high school. What have you been doing with yourself?"

"This is my husband, Thor."

Guy stared at Thor and said, "You don't have to tell me. He's the one I have to talk to."

Thor inquired, "What's so all important that you have to call me out here in the middle of a case?"

"My girl Zeoli knows something about the Blue Scarlet attacks."

"Do you think I can talk to her?"

"Sure. My shift ends in an hour, then I'll take you to meet her."

Later on, the beach, Thor sat on a bolder with his wife Cherry watching the waves crash on a rocks. He turned to Guy and asked, "Okay, when is your girlfriend supposed to show up?"

Guy put his fingers in his mouth and whistled. The wind began to blow, creating a wave that grew larger than all the other waves the closer it came shore. That created a spray off water that swirled around until it formed into a tall slender, Junoesque woman, clad in a light blue lacy gown that rolled down to her feet. She walked up to Guy and gave him a warm hug and kiss then inquired, "Who are your friends, darling?"

"Zeoli Shannon, this is Thor and his lovely wife Cherry."

Thor stood to his feet, took the woman's right hand, and kissed it and said, "I see you are a Mist Maiden, Zeoli Shannon. It is indeed a pleasure to meet you. I hear you know something about the Blue Scarlet attacks."

"Yes. I was on my way to meet my darling one rainy day when I spotted a heavy-set man enter a toy shop on the town green. As I drew closer, I overheard him make a deal with the toy-maker for a dozen blue, grapefruit size blue spheres."

"Do you know when the spheres are to be delivered?"

"Yes. A week from yesterday."

A curious Cherry inquired, "Miss Zeoli. How long can you stay on land?"

"Once I take human form, I can stay on land indifferently. Why do you ask?"

"Oh, no particular reason. I thought because you are a Mist Maiden you would evaporate."

"If that did happen. I would only come back down as rain. Oh, if you are wondering how we would manage when we get married. We will get along just fine."

A short time later, Thor walked in the toy shop with his wife and asked the tall man in his early fifties, "Excuse me Sir, but do you have any spheres the size of a grapefruit?"

The toy man thought then answered, "I have all kinds of balls. What exactly are do you need them for?"

"I want to put a caustic chemical in them, so I can use them to get rid of my competition."

The toy man put a 'CLOSED' signs the door and said, "I am glad they sent someone back, it's gonna take me a week longer than I expected to make those orbs."

"You better have a good reason for the delay."

"I have the chemicals to put in the spheres, but the molding press is down. So, it will be 2 weeks before you can pick up the next shipment."

"You don't care about the number of people that will be killed when the Blue Scarlet is released?"

"Look, all I care about is the money you pay me. Do we have an agreement on the new date or not?"

"Your heartless piece of garbage!" screamed Thor, as he grabbed the toy-maker by his shirt, hauled him over the counter and hurled him into a display of dolls.

"I need time to fix the molding press and I'll have your orbs!" shouted the Toy-maker.

Thor got in the man's face and stated through clenched teeth, "I'm the Galaxy Sentinel. You Half-wit."

The toy-maker turned to flee, Thor grabbed him, lifted him over his head and threw him through the glass door onto the sidewalk. The enraged Thor bent over the man and landed a hard-right cross to the toy-maker's face, shattering his jaw. Cherry touched Thor's back saying, "Hon. Save some pieces for the authorities."

A police officer walked up to Thor and inquired, "What's going on?"

Thor pointed to the Toy-maker and said, "He's been supplying the 12 with the Blue Scarlet Spheres. Lock him up somewhere so he doesn't escape. But I think he'll need surgery on his face first."

"Yes Sir."

Thor entered the toy shop and asked, "Cherry, see if you can find toy toy-maker's contact list."

A middle-aged woman entered the store and asked Thor thinking he was the shop owner. "Could you donate some toys for the children who were caught in those horrible attacks?"

Thor stared at the woman with a forlorn expression on her face and said, "You can have everything you can carry out." The woman rushed away as Cherry handed Thor a Rolodex and pointed to a card.

Thor contacted the 12 and when someone answered he stated firmly, "I have the Toymaker and you are next." Then hung up.

The woman rushed back in the store and asked, "Is your offer still good?"

"Yes. Take it all."

The woman shouted, "Alright boys, everything in the shop is ours!"

Forty minutes later the woman thanked Thor repeatedly for his generosity then left to disturb the toys to the kids. Thor turned to Cherry and said, "It's time to close up the shop for good. Then he heard a little girl ask, "Excuse me Mister but do you have a dolly that I can buy? I lost mine last week when a bad man tried to kill people."

The mother stated, "Don't bother the man because I don't think he has anymore Dolls."

Cherry spotted one doll 18 inched tall doll with golden ringlets in her hair, high on a shelf, climbed the ladder, got the doll, gave it to the little girl and said, "This is for you to have."

The mother offered to pay Cherry for it she said, "No. the doll is free."

The little girl handed the doll to her mother, reached her arms up to Thor. He knelt, the girl threw her arms around Thor's neck, gave him a hug and kiss, saying, "Thank you Mister." and happily walked out of the shop.

Thor stood, turned to his wife, and said, "It is times like this that makes me glad that I'm the Galaxy Sentinel."

As Thor was closing the shop door, a man rushed up to him out of breath and reported, "There is a young girl sitting barely dressed, under a tree on the town green, but she is not moving. The police tried talking to her, but she acts as if she is a manikin."

Thor charged on the scene with Cherry hollering, "Get everybody away from her! There is a Blue Scarlet orb inside her!" Thor touched his computer watch and said, "Rock, I need four men in has-mat suits with gray spore, spraying canisters at my position immediately. I have a Level One Emergency that needs to be contained."

"But what about the young girl?" Cried the concerned police officer.

Thor took his knife, knelt down and cut open the young girls left arm to reveal plant fibers."

Four men in red has-mat suits appeared in a flash of pale blue light, surrounded the replica, and began to spray her with gray spores, just as it exploded, releasing a huge blue toxic cloud.

One of the Institute's men hollered, "Sir, there is something wrong! The gray spores don't seem to be as effective this time."

Thor touched his computer watch and said, "Professor. How soon can you get to my position with 10 gallons of Sodium hydroxide in a sprayer?"

The old professor hobbled out of an open portal, handed Thor the spray tank and said, "Have at it."

Thor put on the spray tank and joined the others and sprayed the deadly cloud with Sodium hydroxide and help neutralize the blue cloud. Thor handed his tank to one of the men and said, "Have the lab mix this with the spores. And thanks for the help guys."

Thor gazed at the dead grass and trees because of the cloud and wondered when it would all end. Just then he caught a glimpse of a heave set man on the far end of the green waving to him. Thor's jaw dropped open in shock and muttered, "But it can't be him. He was killed in his room at the Institute by Prince Blue."

Cherry inquired, "What's wrong Thor? You look as if you see a ghost."

"I just may have."

"Tell me."

"No, it was just my imagination that's all. So, forget it."

One of the men in a mat-suit saluted Thor and reported, "We're all done here, Sir. Is there anything else you need us for?"

"No. But have Dora send a cleanup crew here to take care of this mess."

"Yes Sir." answered the Institute's security guard and left.

Thor took Cherry's hand and strolled to a bench and sat down saying, "Cherry, this is turning out to be one lone day."

"What do you say we take the rest of the day off and have some fun?"

Just then a well-dressed youth walked up to them and handed Thor a note and said, "A fat man gave this to me to give to you." Thor read; do you think Blue killed me? As head of the 12, I have only begun to seek my revenge on you and everyone else."

Thor took out his digital wallet, plugged it in to the young man's and said, "Here you go. Treat your young lady with a delicious meal."

The youth looked at the amount and said, "Thanks Mister!" And left.

Cherry pointed to a man escorting a young woman down the street and questioned, "What's wrong with that picture?"

"I don't know. You tell me. All I see is a nicely dressed couple walking down the street,"

"The guy looks like he's practically dragging her. Now look at the young girl's head how wobbly it is. I think he drugged her and is trying to find a place to rape her."

"I must be getting tired, okay let's check them out."

Cherry muttered, "Hey, where did they go? I took my eyes off them for a second and now they're gone."

"Where were they when you last say them?"

"By that old weapons factory."

"You may be right Cherry. But, let's check the alley way first."

Five minutes later, Thor stated, "He must have gone inside." then entered the abandoned weapons factory display room, spotted a discarded, black spear, some 12 feet long with an 8-inch blade fashioned at one end and said, "Good, a Death Spear. This may come in handy."

Cherry paused and stated, "Listen. Can you hear someone moaning?"

"Sure, can, it's coming from the other side of that door."

Thor slowly opened the door to a lavish bedroom, with a woman's clothes scattered all over the floor and laying on the bed was a young, nude, voluptuous woman, with long silky brown hair. Thor opened the door further and saw the man behind a camera taking pictures of the unconscious, woman. The man turned his head with a jerk, saw Thor and sprinted for the door on the other side of the room. Thor cocked his arm and threw the Death Spear and impaled the man's left thigh, sending him to the floor screaming in pain. Thor approached him and said, "Shut up." and kicked him in the head knocking him out.

Cherry covered the young woman with the bed sheet and stated, "Thor, the good news is he didn't assault her. The bad news is she has been aware of what's been happening to her all along."

"How is she doing otherwise?"

The young woman held the sheet around her as she sat up and stated, "The creep groped me." Then she burst into tear. Cherry held her in her arms and said, "He won't be praying on any more young women."

"They'll most likely let him out on a technicality."

"Not where he is going Ma'am." Thor took out his blue crystal and called Ab saying, "I have a live one for you to study old friend."

A minute later, a tall, thin figure clad in a white robe, with light orange skin, dark blue oval eye and a small slit for a mouth stepped out of a swirling emerald green mist. Thor handed the Death Spear to him and said, "Hopefully my medical staff will be able to help him. Gotta go." and dragged the man back through the green mist.

Thor touched his computer watch and said, "Tippy, I have someone who needs your personal touch."

Tippy walked out of a portal, saw the emotionally shattered young woman, sitting on the bed, took her hands and asked. "What's your name?"

"I'm Amanda."

"I am going to link with your mind and help you forget what just happened to you. Do I have your permission?"

"Yes, you do."

Tippy turned to Thor and said, "Dad, this is between us girls."

"I'll be outside waiting."

Twenty minutes later, Amanda walked up to Thor outside, gave him a pack on his cheek and said, "Thank you ever so much Mr. Sentinel. My boyfriend Jack will be along any minute."

"You two have a pleasant day and here is some money to help." Thor touched his computer watch and said, "Dora, I need you to send a cleanup crew to an old weapons factory at my location. I want every scrap of pepper and wall scribble in that warehouse saved. Then I want all the furniture from the factory, put in the gym. Thor out." he then turned to Cherry and said, "The rest of the day is ours."

CHAPTER 13

Moonbeam on The Loose

Back at the Institute three days later, Thor was in his office when Lacy announced over the intercom, "Sir, you have a video call on line 3."

Thor flipped up the video phone panel and said, "Sergeant Banks, what can I do for you?"

"I hear you shut down a thriving, illegal, pornographic ring in an old weapons factory and took all the evidence with you."

"That's what I normally do when I arrest someone. You have a problem with that?"

"Yes, I have a problem with that! I want the man you caught and the evidence you took back! You do not have the authority to come to this planet and do whatever you want!"

"You want to give me a minute."

"That's all I'll give you."

Thor put the video phone on pause, set the Retrieval Computer for Sergeant Banks's office, picked up a return button and transported himself right in front of Sergeant Banks. Stuck his finger in his face and stated firmly, "You're the new kid on the block so I'll cut you some slack. I am the Galaxy Sentinel and my authority is the whole galaxy. Which means my authority is supersedes yours. We either work together, or you find yourself a new job. Any questions?"

"No, Sir." whispered Banks.

I thought so. Now if you will excuse me I have better things to do than stand here and talk to you." Thor pressed his Retrieval button and was back in his office in seconds. Thor left his office and went to the gym to go over the stuff that was confiscated from the factory but found the gym empty. Saw Cherish working out in a sweat suit and asked, "Cherish, would you happen to know what happened to the furniture from the weapon's factory is?"

"Moonbeam had a huge warehouse built at the north end of the housing project for that sort of thing."

"Thanks, oh a Cherish, your sweat suit has a big hole in the seat."

She grinned at Thor and backed out of the gym. Thor tapped the intercom and announced, "Will Moonbeam please report to the gym."

Ten minutes later, Moonbeam sauntered in the gym clad in a bright yellow slack suit and asked, "What's up, Chief? I only have five minutes because, I plan to go swimming."

"Where is the furniture from the factory?"

"I had it moved to our new warehouse. Why?"

Who told you to do that?"

"I figured since we had the building, we might as well use it."

"And who gave you permission to build the warehouse?"

"I just assumed, Sir."

"You assumed. Who runs this top-secret facility? You or me?"

"You do Sir."

"Which means you did things without checking with me first!"

"Sorry Sir."

"Is that all you can say is sorry? I run this place Moonbeam, not you! Since you are going swimming I presume you a have a bathing suit on underneath your clothes. So, strip down to your bathing-suit and give me 20 laps around this gym."

"But Sir, I."

"No buts, now, Moonbeam!"

The sprite took off her clothes, grumbling, "This is embarrassing." folded her clothes in a neat pile and jogged in her yellow shorts and a sleeveless silk top."

Cherry walked up to Thor, stared at Moonbeam and inquired, “Why is she running around the gym in her skivvies?”

Thor stared at Moonbeam and answered, “She’s in her underwear? It doesn’t look like it to me. I just finished chewing her out for taking things into her own hands. I figured since she was going to go swimming, she had her suit on underneath her clothes and I told her to give me 20 laps in her bathing suit for her actions.”

“So, what are you going to do now? Embarrass her in front all the men at the Institute?”

“No. Lock the gym doors and let no one in until after she finished her laps and is dressed.”

As Moonbeam jogged passed Cherry, she noticed there was blood on the right cheek. Cherry hollered. “Moonbeam come back here.”

The sprite jugged around the gym, stopped in front of Cherry jogged in place and inquired, “What’s up?”

“Why is there blood on your long johns?”

“The band aid must have fallen off. I sat down in the Arboretum and got a splinter in my tosh. It is no big deal.”

“Did you see Chrissy about it?”

“With the sprite security, building the tram and warehouse I have no time for Chrissy.”

“Let me see it.”

Moonbeam stood still, stared up at Thor, and said, “If you don’t mind giving me some privacy. With Thor’s back turned the sprite turned around opened the butt flap and bent over. Cherry gasped and said, “That is infected! Report to Chrissy right now and have it looked after.”

“I can’t, Doc. is gone for the day.”

Thor suggested, “Why don’t we take the tram to the beach, then bring her to our place and take care of it ourselves.”

Moonbeam turned back around, looked up at Thor and said, “I am so sorry for taking thing into my own hands, and I promise it won’t happen again.”

“You are forgiven, get dressed.”

At Thor's cottage, Moonbeam lay on her bed clad in her union suit Cherry opened the butt flap, and pulled the splinter out, then dabbed a hot tea on the infected wound."

Moonbeam inquired, "How many treatments am I going need?"

"Twice a day for three days should take care of the infection. Oh, Thor will be dabbing the tea on your rump, I am going to be busy."

"No absolutely not. I will not show your husband my bare tushy."

"Just pulling your wings Moonbeam. Be here for breakfast and dinner so I can take care of you and no buts about it."

"Not funny, Mrs. T."

Belinda walked in the house, handed Thor a stack of bank stubs and said, "By the looks like these stubs, this pervert that was taking pictures of nude women and was using the money to support the 12." and left the room.

"I want the address of his clients. This pornography ring is going down." Thor poked his head in the bedroom and asked, "Is it alright to come in?"

"Come on it Hon, Moonbeam is decent."

"Why don't we have Moonbeam sleep on the couch until the infection is cleared up? I'll have Pixy fill in for her as head of security until her butt is healed."

"Thank you, Sir. Oh, Sir, can you open your shirt for me? I need to do something."

Moonbeam turned to Cherry and asked, "Can you hold the towel around me, so your husband doesn't get a peek at me." Moonbeam sat up, placed her hand on Thor's bare chest saying, "I can find out a lot about a person by just touching them. She closed her eyes and concentrated for two minutes and said, "I understand your position as head if the Institute. But may I suggest? Let Sergeant Banks be in charge of the raids in shutting down the porno ring."

"Excellent idea," stated Thor as he stared at Moonbeam and questioned, "What were you going to use for a bathing suit?"

Moonbeam grimaced and said, "I usually swim in my clothes. It's fun."

Thor stared at the sprite and said, "Ahh, yeah." Thor then asked, "When Governor Victor met you on the tundra that day and beat you and left you for dead. Did you have those scars taken care of?"

"Yes Sir."

"Then tell me why you are afraid to show your arms and legs to people?"

"Because I like to be modest. Is there a crime against that?" snapped Moonbeam.

Thor directed, "Moonbeam, take off your union suit if you please."

Moonbeam held unto her ground hollering, "I am not going to let you see me naked!"

Thor sat on the bed next to the sprite and said in a soft voice, "Your part of the Institute family and I want to help you."

Moonbeam turned around, unbuttoned her long underwear, lowered it to her coccyx and showed Thor her marred body.

Thor asked, "Did Governor Victor do that to you when he beat you?"

With tears in her eyes, Moonbeam nodded her head yes, then said, "I figured I had to live the rest of my life looking like a monster. So, I covered up my scars and prayed no one would see them. That's why I didn't go to Dr. Chrissy. I didn't want her to see my hideous body."

"Chrissy can take care of those scars for you."

"She can?" asked the sprite with a flicker of hope in her eyes.

"Just ask Belinda."

Moonbeam fell into Thor's arms crying, as Belinda walked back in the room, gazed at her father and Moonbeam, and inquired, "Mom. Why is Dad hugging Moonbeam half naked?"

Moonbeam let go of Thor, covered herself, faced Belinda and stated, "I just found out I can get rid of my scars."

"You are going to have the surgery? Far out! Hey, let me show you a few photos of what I looked like before my operation."

"Do you mind if I get dressed first?" asked Moonbeam. She stared at Thor and said, "You, out."

"Time to make some Coconut-Hazelnut coffee," stated Thor walking out of the bedroom.

Sometime later, sitting in a bamboo chair, on the front porch, Thor was nursing his coffee, contacted Sergeant Banks, and stated, "Sergeant, that man I caught today is Paul Rosenburger. He was using the money he made from those porno photos to support the 12. I am sending you the addresses of all Paul's clientele. I expect you to set up a task force and shut them down."

"Do you think Paul's clients are supporting the 12 also?"

"It's a good possibility."

"Excellent, I'll get on it right away. Sergeant Banks, out."

Thor opened a large manila folder took out the nude pictures of Amanda and studied the photo of her laying on her stomach. Tippy sat next to her father and asked, "Dad, why are you looking at Amanda's nude picture?"

"I am not drooling over them, I'm looking at the tattoo of a Leopard just above her tailbone."

"Didn't each of the Leopard street gang have one of those tattoos?"

"Sure did. All twelve members of the Leopards were androids designed to create a vortex that would destroy a solar system. But what bothers me is where the detonator was."

"I linked with her mind, Dad and she seemed human to me. I don't know. She could she be the detonating device."

Thor put the pictures back in the folder and said, "Tippy. Put these where no one will find them. Then somehow, bring in Amanda in for questioning. I'll contact Mike and Heather and tell him to call Teeny and Cindy that I need them."

"Do you have a plan Dad?"

"If I miss my guess, I think I will be able to use Amanda to take out The Dreaded 12."

"I'll have her here in no time, Dad." Tippy gave Thor a kiss and flew off.

Cherry sat next to Thor, gave him a fresh mug of coffee. Horatio lit on the porch rail in front of Thor and stated, "You better make fast tracks for the Institute. One of the sprites has flipped their wig."

Ten minutes later, Thor met 3 sharpshooters in the hall just outside the cafeteria waiting for the right moment to take out Todd. Thor ordered, "Stand down. I'll take care of this, pushed open the door to the cafeteria, saw Todd dressed in a green striped hospital gown, holding a knife to Missy's throat hollering, "No one leaves here until someone brings me Mary Bell!"

"What do you want Mary Bell for?" inquired Thor.

Todd pressed the point of the knife against sprite Missy's side saying, "That's none of your business Thor! Now, bring Mary Bell here or I'll shove this knife in Missy!"

Thor took a step towards Todd praying he wouldn't hurt Missy. Todd shoved the knife in the sprite's side two inches, causing her to cry out in pain. Todd shouted, "One more step and I'll cut her open! You have ten minutes to bring Mary Bell here before Missy dies!"

Missy mustered all her strength, positioned her head, opened her mouth, and bit Todd's forearm. He dropped Missy and let out a scream. Thor dove forward, tackling Todd. Chrissy rushed in to tend to Missy's wound as Thor touched his watch and said, "King Mex. I have Todd in custody."

Sprite Charlotte rushed up to bound Todd on the floor clad in a lovely blue gingham dress that went down to her knees. Knelt by his side and wiped the sweat from Todd's face. He looked at her and asked, "Charlotte you're beautiful. What did you do?"

"I gave my life to Christ and He cleaned me up inside. Charlotte helped Todd to a chair saying "Let Mary Bell go because she is married to Jay. All I want you to do is help you to get better, so we can spend our lives together."

"Will I see you tomorrow?" asked Todd not believing what Charlotte told him.

"King Mex has a prayer meeting in the jail, I'll meet you there." Charlotte put her arms around Todd, kissed him and said, "You don't have to go through this alone. I'll be with you all the way."

A much gentler Todd glanced at Thor and asked, "Can I speak to Missy?"

"Sure."

Todd locked his gaze on Missy and asked, "Will you forgive me for what I did to you?"

"Sure, I forgive you." Missy then shouted, "Does anybody have a Bible they can give Todd?"

CHAPTER 14

More Clues

After Todd was taken away, Thor asked, Berry the cook, "Give me a cup of coffee." He tuned to the staff in the cafeteria and stated, "Todd did not struggle against the brainwashing, he had Gus give it to him of his own free will."

A staff member stood up and inquired, "What can we do to support Todd?"

"Send him cards, letter, visit him when you can and be a morale support for Charlotte." Thor picked up one of Missy's favorite sandwiches from the kitchen and a cup of tea, headed for the infirmary and handed it to Missy saying, "I thought you might like this."

The sprite's eyes widened with excitement and hollered, "Oh boy! A sardine and peanut sandwich and Chamomile tea, Thanks Boss."

Thor walked in his office and asked, "Lacy, have Cathy come to my office."

"She is in there waiting for you right now."

Thor opened the door, saw Cathy, and said, "I hope you have good news for me concerning the missing women."

"It all depends what you call good news."

"That's not what I want to hear Cathy."

"I found the twelve women that match the DNA you gave me. But they are all dead."

"Are you telling me The Dreaded Twelve murdered those women in cold blood?"

"No Sir."

"Then what are you saying?"

"I scanned the Dark Planet's moon three times and found nothing. What I think is going on here is those twelve missing women never existed. Because those twelve women are alien females from Montros who disguised themselves as Human women. Went to Queen Diane and suggested that she start the Palaces Scouts. The reason is they wanted to learn about humans' weakness without being detected. When they were ready the women went to the Dead Forest became The Dreaded Twelve and attacked people with the Blue Scarlet, using the kidnapped women to keep the upper hand."

"Excellent idea, but now I have to prove it. But as for you Cathy, take a few days off and soak up some sun."

Thor tapped the intercom and said, "Lacy, tell my wife that she is to be ready to leave for Diane's plaice within the hour."

Mary Bell entered the office with her baby, Alisha Bell and asked, "Can I have a few of my people hand out flyers at the Tram stations?"

"Sure, advertising your encouragement group?"

"All I do is get the saints to focus on the cross of Christ for all their problems. You want to hold Alisha Bell, so I can visit my sister Missy?"

"Sure, take your time."

Forty minutes later, Thor handed the baby back to Mary Bell saying, "I think she needs changing." He touched the intercom and said, "Lacy, get me the Mystery's Three for me." A Minute later, Lace announced over the intercom, "Mystery's Three on video line 3."

Thor flipped up the blue video phone cover and asked the woman, on the view screen that had short, brown hair in her thirties,

"Trudy, I'll get right to the point. I need you three to dig up some information on twelve women."

"We are backed up concerning jobs. But I can spare you Debbie if you like."

"That's great, tell her to meet Cherry and me on the Dark Planet's moon, in the Phoenix cafe in Nautikos city, two hours."

"Will do, Oh, just FYI, the original name for the Dark Planet before it was taken over after the down fall of the Tealing Empire three hundred years ago, was called, Adinidiin or pronounced, Doo ndaaz dah and congratulations on you, being appointed Alien Ambassador. Trudy out."

Cherry entered the office dressed in jeans and a green short sleeve shirt and inquired, "I heard we are going pay another visit to the Queen? You've got the hots for her?"

"Of course, not Cherry. I don't go around chasing other women."

"Relax Sweet. I'm just having fun with you."

"Cathy thinks the kidnapped women are in reality the Dreaded Twelve from Montros. So, we have to go back and look for evidence to prove that they are Renegades,"

"Cool beans. I'm already, and so is Gideon Bear."

Thor parked the Star car in the parking lot, on the right side of a nineteen-fifty's styles diner that had a three-dimensional replica of the Phoenix rising out of the ashes over it. Cherry kissed Thor and said, "I have to powder my nose, find a booth and I'll see you in a bit."

A pudgy woman, clad in a burgundy slack suit, with curly reddish-brown hair in her mid-twenties, carrying a tan back pack full of equipment sat down and said, "Hi, I'm Debbie. You wanted to see me?"

"We need to go to the plaice and look for anything that will tell us that those 12 women are from Montros."

"Where those women in a barracks or did they have individual rooms?" questioned Debbie.

"Each woman had their own room, why do you ask?"

"So, I know how much time it's going to take me to look for the clues, 12 rooms, means a lot of work are you willing to pay a large amount?"

"Whatever it takes to bring these women down money is no object."

"Enough with the business it's time to put on the old feed bag because, I'm going to have some strawberry pancakes sausages and an omelet what about you, Thor?"

Cherry walked up to the booth, glared at Debbie, and snapped, "He'll have the same as I'm having, house special."

Debbie threw her hands up saying, "Retract the claws lady. I'm on your side."

After the waitress served everyone coffee, Thor looked at his wife and asked, "Do you want to tell me what's has you on the attack?"

"You want to explain this?" and showed Thor an intimate picture of him and Rose in the hot springs.

"Where did you get this?"

"It was given to me just before we left."

Debbie glanced at the photo and asked, "Give me that for a minute? Maybe I can shed some light on the subject." Debbie placed a white, six inch by twelve-inch sheet of plastic on the table, touched in on the upper left side, then slip the photo of Thor and Rose underneath it. The white plastic turned transparent and Debbie stated, "Computer, scan the photo for discrepancies."

The computer stated, "There are 2."

Debbie gazed at Cherry and said, "You have been fooled by a composite picture. Somebody took a photo of Rose in the hot spring without her knowing it, put Thor's head on someone body and put him next to Rose."

Thor inquired, "Hon, where did you get this?"

"Like I said somebody gave it to me in an envelope before we left"

"Why didn't you say something to me about it sooner? You know I would never cheat on you Cherry." Thor touched his computer watch and said, "Abbie. I want you to find out who's spreading the rumor about me cheating on Cherry. Then, check to see if you can find a hidden camera in the trees around the woman's hot springs. But don't say anything until I get back."

"Will do, Dad. Abbie out."

At the Palace, Diane showed Debbie the rooms where the 12-woman stayed and said, "The rooms have never been touched, since their kidnapping."

Thor shook Debbie's hand saying, "Good luck in your search. Cherry and I have to go to Montros to check on a few things. Is there anything you need, before we go?"

"No. But thanks for asking."

Thor landed the star car in front of a free standing grey stone building in the middle of a grassy meadow and said, "This is the Face Master's place, I want all his records packed in the trunk of the car. Hopefully we will find a clue as to whom the Dreaded Twelve are."

Cherry put Gideon on her shoulders and followed Thor inside and began to pack the pictures on the wall. Gideon waddled up to a panel on the wall and tapped it with his paw.

Cherry hollered, "Thor, Gidester found something."

"It still amazes me how a computer-generated bear can do so much." Thor examined the panel and said, "I can't find a trip lever or switch. I guess there is only one thing left to do." Thor doubled up his fist and rammed it through the wall paneling, then ripped off and threw it on the floor, to find a wall safe. Thor set his energy pistol to a fine beam, cut the safe open. Then took out twelve pictures of Montronian females who had themselves transformed into human women. All the specks on each of them, human and Montroinan were there alone with their human names. Thor then stared at the information of the one who paid The Face Master the sixteen thousand Druxes.

Cherry inquired "What's wrong Thor? You look as if you just seen a ghost."

"I have. Look at the man behind The Dreaded Twelve."

"It can't be him. I saw Big Blue kill that sicko."

"Pack the rest of this stuff in the car, then we have to pay a visit to Isidro Hayes, or the Face Master."

"As soon as I take this stuff out to the car, we will go."

When Thor walked back in the building he met two Montronians, one had Cherry pinned against a counter trying to get to second base. While other one had his right foot on Gideon's back, pinning him face down on the floor. Thor calmly stated, "Sirs, get your hands off my wife and let the bear go if you know what's good for you."

The one struggling with Cherry, spun her around, put his left arm across her chest, pulled her close to him then stuck his knife to her stomach saying, "Leave now, and I won't kill her."

Thor grabbed the man's hand and pulled it away from Cherry allowing her to escape, then swiftly he shoved the knife in his stomach. The one holding Gideon down tried to make a quick retreat. Thor yanked the knife out of the dead man, and threw it, hitting him in his back. Cherry pulled her blouse closed, fell into Thor's arms saying, "I am glad you came in when you did. I don't think I could have held that pervert off too much longer."

"What happened?"

"They seem to come out of nowhere; one pinned Gidester, while the other grabbed me, kissed me, and ripped my blouse open trying to cop a feel. I know one thing, I am not going to wear these braless blouses anymore."

"Shall we go for a mug of goheeh before we talk to Isiy?"

"Ah Hon, Sweetheart, I can't go outside like this. Could you please get my booby catcher and other blouse I have in the trunk of the star car?"

"You keep a change of clothes in the car? I didn't know that."

"Yes. Now hurry up before someone comes in and sees me like this."

"What's wrong with the way you are right now?" quipped Thor.

"Just get me a top to wear."

Thor held Cherry in his arms and said, "There is an office over there where we can have some privacy."

"I don't want to be caught like this now, get me my blouse."

Thor emerged from the office with his wife, 70 minutes later with Cherry smiling from ear to ear, clad in a blue red and yellow dress and said, "Who'd thought this guy would have a closet full of women's clothes and thanks Hon for suggesting some personal time together. Hey, you open the trunk and I'll grab an armload of dressed, because I am not going to let them go to waste."

Twelve minutes later, Cherry had packed the trunk full of clothes, Thor stared at her and questioned, "What in the world are you going to do with all those clothes?"

"Give most of them to the women on staff and the rest to the church. Are we still up for that cup of coffee, ah, excuse me, goheeh?"

In a small cafe, a short distance from the police station, Thor and his wife sat in a booth nursing a mug of hot goheeh. Cherry inquired, "Do you think Woody is behind these Blue Scarlet attacks? I don't. I think someone is trying to pull a fast one."

Just then, a 6-foot-tall man, with short blond hair, clad in fancy clothes sat next to Cherry, placed his hand on her thigh saying, "I am glad to see you two are healthy."

Cherry growled, "Remove your hand before you lose it, Dirtbag."

"You wound me to the quick Cherry. I came in here to give you a chance to save the Alliance from total annihilation, by Blue Scarlet, as you call it. But I like to refer it as a fast way to get rid of a lot of people all at once."

Thor grabbed Woody by his shirt, hauled him over the table and stated, "So you are the one who has been slaughtering all those people in cold blood."

"Hey, don't kill the messenger."

"What about those twelve Montroinan women you had changed to look human?"

"I've been framed. Besides, you can't do anything to me without the proper evidence and right now all you have is, nothing. So, let go of the threads before I sue you for a new set of clothes."

Thor threw Woody on the floor and said, "I'll give you just thirty seconds to get out of my sight."

Woody stood to his feet and questioned, "Or, what?"

Cherry stood up, kneed Woody where it hurt the most sending him on the floor groaning in pain and stated, "If you even think of touching me, again, I'll make sure you sing soprano for the rest of your life!"

CHAPTER 15

Woody's Back

At the police station an hour later, Thor approached the desk clerk and inquired, "I like to see Isidro P. Hayes."

"I'll have him escorted to room 6 so you can question him."

In room 6, Thor walked up to Hayes handcuffed to his chair and asked, "What do you know about Woody?"

"Woody? Who is he?"

"Don't get cute with me Isidro, I have the order for the photos and the payment receipt from Woody. Why did he want twelve Montros woman changed into human females?"

"I don't ask my customers what they plan to do when I transform them into humans. I take their money and give them what they want. One couple even had me change their infant, go figure."

Thor grabbed the hair on the back of Isidro's head, slammed his face on the table 4 times, and then bellowed, "Wrong answer! What does Woody plan to do with those twelve women?"

Isidro wiped the blood from his nose and said, "Woody made a call on his computer watch to someone and said something about mixing a slimy blue fungus with other chemicals to increase its potency and a smear campaign to destroy the Institute. Oh, don't try to do a DNA scan for them because Woody and the woman have DNA scramblers."

"What about the Planetary Alliance?"

"Woody is going to use the Alliance to destroy the Institute and he doesn't care how many people he has to kill to do it."

"Thank you,"

"For what? Ending my life. Because that is what is going to happen to me once Woody finds out I finked in him."

Thor touched his computer watch and said, "Rock, send two of your men to my location. A midget by the name of Isidro P. Hayes needs protection." Thor turned to his wife and said, "It's time we headed for home. Where's Gidester?"

Cherry cringed, "I think I packed him in the trunk along with the rest of the clothes."

Thor opened the trunk of the star car, saw the blue bear's paw sticking out of a green dress, pulled him out and said, "Sorry, Squirt."

Back at the Institute, Thor instructed sprite Misty, "I know it is late in the evening, but can you find out how the Tram depots are doing? Then report to me."

"Does that mean, you're appointing me General Supervisor of the whole shebang, Sir?"

"You've got it."

"Yes! When do you need the report, Sir?"

"You can give it to me tomorrow morning."

Misty gathered the reports from the Tram Depot Managers, went home, took a shower, slipped into her bathrobe and slippers then made herself a cup of herbal tea.

Sprite Todd, strolled out of a nearby closet, clad in jeans, red shirt with a knife strapped to his belt. Misty took a deep breath, smiled and inquired, "Did King Mex let you go? Would you like a cup of hot tea? I just made some." glanced at her sleeping pills, slipped one in Todd's drink, and gave his tea.

Minutes later, Todd put down his empty cup, picked up his knife, and a package wrapped in brown paper, took hold of Misty's arm, brought her into the bedroom then instructed, "Get rid of your robe and get in bed!"

"But I don't have anything on underneath my robe."

"I don't care! Now do as I say!" Shouted Todd, gripping his knife firmly in his right hand.

Misty tried to remain calm as she climbed into bed, then took off her robe, wondering what Todd was going to do next. Misty stared at the package on the nightstand as Todd joined her in bed as she questioned, "Is that a present for someone?" Misty took a slow deep breath, smiled sheepishly and stated, "If you are thinking about going for a home run with me. I have an infection. Ah, just FYI." she then held Todd's hand to keep him calm.

When Misty though Todd, was asleep, she touched her computer watch and whispered, "Cherry, Todd forced me in bed with him at knife point. He also has a package that might be a bomb."

"What is he doing now?"

"Sleeping next to me in bed with his knife in his hand."

"Try to keep him busy until we get there."

"I'll see what I can do without losing my purity as a lady sprite."

Todd suddenly opened his eyes, threw his right leg on top of Misty, and held the knife to her throat with a fierce look in his eyes and stated, "You are going to do as I say or else."

Misty looked up at Todd and said, "Are you going to blow us up?"

"That's none of your business."

Misty sighed and thought, there is only way to stop him, then she said, "If you want to go for it. I won't stop you." then placed her hands-on Todd's bare back, closed her eyes and cringed, expecting Todd take her up on her offer.

Blood slowly trickled down the side of Misty's throat as Todd added pressure to the knife hollering, "You're just like all the other women Mary Bell, you take from a guy and dump them! Well no more! You and everyone else are going to pay for what you did to me!"

"But I'm Misty, not Mary Bell."

"Shut up you stupid Trollop!"

Misty began to massage Todd's back causing him to relax, and let go of the knife, she then said, "If you roll over on your stomach, I will give you a body rub you won't forget." tears silently rolled down

Misty cheeks as she looked up at the poster of a kitten she had on the ceiling, trying to remain calm, wondering what Todd was going to do to her.

Todd smiled, kissed Misty on her lips, she glared up at him, dug her fingernails in his back screaming, "Stop right there, Mister! You have to be my husband to continue!"

Todd, flew in a rage, grabbed Misty by the throat, ready to drive the knife in her chest. Thor and Cherry raced in the bedroom, Thor grabbed Todd and threw him to the floor and dragged him off screaming at Misty at the top of his lungs.

Cherry placed a gauze on Misty's throat and asked, "Are you alright?"

"I wish you would have showed up two minutes earlier."

"Did ah, Todd do it to you?"

"He was about to, but I stopped him before he could. Misty hung her head and confessed, "Cherry, I have got to tell you this. Joe and I blew it big time, a week ago. We didn't mean to, it was all my fault. We were over my place horsing around in the Living room. The next thing I knew, it happened. Boy, did I feel like crap after."

Misty put on her robe as Joe rushed in, gave her a hug saying, "When I heard what happened, I was so scared Todd was going to kill you."

"I am fine Joe, thanks to Thor and Cherry."

Thor instructed, "Cherry get everyone out the house, the package contains a bomb and enough Blue Scarlet, to takeout this whole neighborhood and is set to go off any minute."

"I'm on it Hon," stated Cherry rushing out the door to sound the alarm.

The next morning, Thor walked in the huge blue and white warehouse by the housing project and hollered, "Hey, Teeny! You in here?"

"Behind the white partition on the far left side!"

Thor poked his head around the dividers, saw parts of the android Amanda everywhere and inquired, "How are things going?"

"Amanda is one of the most fascinating androids I have ever seen. I managed to shut her down, disconnect her arms legs and head. Now I am trying to figure out how to open her torso. I have poked, prodded and pressed everything I can think of and I still can't open her up."

"Have you thought about sticking your finger in her bellybutton?"

Teeny chuckled and asked, "You are kidding me. Right?"

"It's worth a try."

Teeny stuck his right index finger in Amanda's navel as far as it could go, that loosened the top half of her body. Teeny lifted it off and exclaimed, "Whoa! This is gonna take a while. I have never seen so many gizmos in one android in all my life." Teeny pointed to a dark red ball the size of a baseball loaded with little knobs and remarked, "That has to be the triggering device. But, getting it out is going to be something else."

"By the way, where is Cindy?" inquired Thor.

"She's most likely looking over your new tram system. Talk to you later, I have tons of work to do."

Horatio flew up to Thor, landed on his shoulder, and reported, "Sir. Your presence is needed in the Beach Tram station, right away. You will have to use the emergency entrance, Thor took the elevator down then walked through the tube to get the location because the tram system is shut down."

Thor walked out of the tram tube, saw a group of people gathered around Mary Bell sitting on one of the platform benches with a brown package in her hands crying. He made his way through the crowd and asked, "What's wrong Mrs. Bright?"

"Don't come near me!" screamed the tearful sprite, trembling.

Thor turned to Constance and said, "Clear the tram stations of people and seal all shafts leading to the surface."

"The ventilation seats too?"

"Yes, now move it!" Thor then announced, "The tram stations are closed until further notice. Please make your way to the surface as quickly as possible." Thor turned to Mary Bell Bright and asked,

"You want to tell me what's wrong and why you are holding that package in your hands?"

"I woke up this morning and Jay and my babe were gone with a note in my hand that said, I had to take this package to this tram station and wait. If I didn't, Jay and Alisha Bell would be killed."

"Can you give me the parcel?"

With tears streaming down her cheeks, Marry Bell cried, "Please leave, Sir. I don't want you to die too."

Horatio hopped up to Thor and said, "The package contains five pounds of Blue Scarlet powder with a triggering device attached to the side of the box. As soon as Mrs. Bell let's go, the deadly blue powder will be released. And I don't have to tell you the catastrophic events that will follow."

"What do you propose we do?"

"I'll inform Rock to have his men get ready to spray the Blue Scarlet with the gray spores when it comes out of the shafts."

"You do that, bird. Then find Jay and Alisha. Now go!"

"They are right here." stated Cindy.

Android Cindy walked up to Mary Bell, knelt down and instructed, "I am going to slide my hands under yours slowly. I want you to try and keep as much pressure on the detonation switch as possible."

Once Cindy had the deadly package in her hands Mary Bell slowly rose to her feet to join her family. Cindy looked at Thor and said, "I need someone to bend a sturdy, flat piece of metal that will hold the sides of the package."

Once the metal clamp was in place, Cindy opened a vortex to the nearest sun and threw it in, destroying it.

Mary Bell, gave her baby to Jay, walked up to Thor, looked up at him, promptly turned around, bent over, and said, "Go ahead Sir, I deserve a good swift kick in my sit-down for what I almost did."

Thor gave Mary Bell a tap on her butt with his hand saying, "Straighten up and face me and take your punishment."

The sprite, stood at attention expecting the worst, Thor swept her up in his arms and said, "What you need is a big hug, and some time off in Willow City where you will be safe."

"Thank you, thank you, thank you." Mary Bell took her babe and her husband in hand saying, "Come on Love Muffin, let's go have some fun in the city!"

That night Thor clasped on the front porch, with a cup of Coconut-Hazelnut coffee and asked his wife, "Cherry. How did a postal package get by our scanners?"

"It could have come from someone right here on the planetoid. But then, our scanners should have picked up that much Blue Scarlet."

Sam walked on the porch with his wife Dora, a five foot five inches tall, fifty-five years old woman who weighs two hundred and twenty pounds. Cherry jumped up saying, be right back with your coffees."

Sam stated, "I heard there was a little excitement this evening."

"We had two Blue Scarlet attacks. First Misty, then Mary Bell. They are both okay, but for the life of me I can't figure out where the attacks are coming from. Sam, I want you to send the GS-2 Squad to the dark planet's moon and dig more information on the supposed kidnapped women. I think they are in reality The Dreaded Twelve."

Sam thanked Cherry for his coffee and asked, "How did you come up with that conclusion?"

"Woody had The Face Master change 12 Montronian women into humans. The 12 Palace's women scouts are Renegades. One of the Scouts was murdered, and the body was sent to the palace. Have the Queen exhume the body and do a DNA match."

Dora took a swallow of her coffee and stated, "Moonbeam had surgery today to remove her scars and she is doing fine. She should be back to work in three weeks. Miss Puckett from the lab wants to see you first thing in the morning about synthesizing some blue fungus."

Cherry quietly excuse herself then came out later with a birthday cake for Dora followed by Belinda with an arm load of presents for her.

Sam inquired, "Thor. What are we going to do with Todd? He almost killed Misty twice and a lot of innocent people. If you want my opinion I think we should vaporize him and be done with it. He is a menace to society."

"I know he has escaped from King Mex twice so far. I'll give Ab a call in the morning and see what he can do."

Cherry stated, "Enough with the chatter, I want to see what Dora got for her birthday."

CHAPTER 16

The Dead Forest Melee

The next morning, Thor set a blue crystal on his desk, contacted Ab and said, "I need your help. I have a sprite that is a danger to himself and everyone around him. I was wondering if you could help him."

"Be there in a jiff."

Two minutes later a small swirling green mist appeared in Thor's office that steadily grew until it was 8 feet in diameter. Then out walked Ab clad in a light blue robe, with someone clad in a white robe and said, "Thor, you know Doctor Eb. He's here to treat Todd."

Thor touched the intercom and said, "Security, bring Todd into my office."

Seven minutes later two security guards dragged the sprite in struggling and screaming obscenities. Eb took a skullcap out of his medical bag, slipped it over Todd's head and immediately the sprite calmed down. Eb stated, the computer circuitry in the skullcap will keep him in a passive state. Then once a week I will hook the cap up to a computer and unscramble his brain."

"I suppose you will lock him up in some asylum somewhere on your planet."

"On, no Sir. Todd will be staying at a campground with other people like him and will get the best of care."

"He is all yours Doctor. Charlotte charged in Thor's office, threw her arms around Todd, and begged to go with him.

Eb, thought for a moment then said, "It is highly irregular, but the woman's love just might be the thing he need to bring him back. Come along ma'am."

Miss Puckett rushed in Thor's off all out of breath, with a large metal container in her hands and inquired, "You'll never guess what I have in here?"

"You're right. Now tell me."

"You know that sample of blue fungus you sent me?" I can synthesized as much as we need."

"Okay, now that we have an abundance of blue fungus what are we going to do with it?"

"I can combine the fungus with the gray spores and accelerate the destruction of a Blue Scarlet attack."

"That is great news. How many Spray canisters can you have ready by noon?"

"About 5 canisters why do you ask?"

"The way things are going these days, I don't want to be left high and dry during a Blue Scarlet attack."

"I'll stockpile a few more canisters so we can have a ready supply. Gotta go Sir."

Thor walked into the cafeteria, poured himself a mug of coffee and sat in a booth in the back-left corner. Cherry sat next to him a few minutes later and asked, "What's been happening in your world l today?"

"Trying to figure out how to get on top of all these attacks."

Rose walked up, and sat opposite Thor and stated, "I have to talk to you two about Fara. I was talking to her the other day and noticed she was upset about something, but, she would not tell me what."

Cherry thought for a moment then inquired, "Do you think Fara is into something she shouldn't be?"

"You mean is Fara fooling around with men?"

"I don't think so. But there is something bothering her."

"Cherry and I will speak to her today." Thor took out a nude photo of him and Rose and in the hot springs, showed it to Rose and stated, "When the women on my staff start posing for nude photos, it's time they found another job."

"Where did you get this picture from?" questioned a shocked Rose.

"It was shoved under Cherry's door this morning."

Rose studied the picture then said, "This was taken in the Acceleration System."

"How can you tell?" inquired Thor.

"The formation of the rocks around the hot springs are different and that is not me. It's a three-dimensional image of me and a poor one at that."

Cherry studied the photo and said, "Rose, you are right, your butt is bigger, but who would do a thing like this?"

"Probably the same person who is attacking the Alliance and I do not have a big keister."

Debbie walked up to the booth, sat next to Rose and reported, "I found Montronian DNA in all twelve of the woman's rooms. Now get this. I found a memo from Woody telling the women where to go for their scouting trip and they should be called themselves The Dreaded Twelve."

"That's what I needed to link Woody to; the twelve women from the planet Montros."

Cherry spoke up and asked, "What I want to know is who has been stirring things up around here?"

"A copycat?"

"The packages Todd had looked like it was sent through the mail. So, it still could be Woody."

Debbie placed a medical report of the exhumed body on the table and stated, "You were right. That murdered woman of the Dreaded Twelve you sent back was not one of the Women Scouts. She was a 35-year-old woman by the name of Miss Andrea Payne from the planet Kylee. She was vacationing in the city when she was reported missing. The autopsy report says that Miss Payne was grabbed from behind and stabbed in the chest by someone much shorter than her. Since Woody is 6 feet and Miss Andrea Payne was 5 feet 7 that leaves him out. Oh, here are the twelve names of the supposedly kidnapped women."

Just then three women rushed up to Thor all dressed in, black with long black capes. The tall one Gamma reported, "GS-2 reporting in Sir. The women you sent us to check on. There are 12 life signs in the Dead Forest all Montronian. But, there is something strange about the life signs that I think needs investigation."

"Thanks. I'll get Sam and we'll check it out. What I want you ladies to do is find Woody and keep an eye on him."

"Will do Sir. Gotta go."

Cherry grabbed Thor's hand saying, "Just one minute husband of mine. You go nowhere without me."

Thor touched his computer watch saying, "Sam, meet me on the Retrieval Computer pad ready to go within thirty minutes. We have to go back to the Dead Forest." Thor turned to his wife and said, "Put your Mysterious Garb on, because we are going in stealth mode."

Sprite Mini hurried up to Cherry and said, "Ma'am, Mrs. Bright is in the Arboretum by the falls crying."

Cherry kissed Thor saying, "I'll meet you in a few minutes, I want to see what's bothering Mary Bell."

Cherry approached the sorrowful sprite back by the fall, sat on the grass with her and asked, "You want to tell me what's wrong? Jay and you have your first fight?"

Eyes red from crying, Mary Bell stated, "There are times I am fine. Then something reminds me of what Todd and Wilfred did to me and the vivid pictures come screaming through my mind as if it happened yesterday ripping and tearing at me like some wild animal."

Cherry stated, "I understand sometimes we have to walk out our healing. But remember, our faith is in Christ, through what he did on the Cross, the power is through the Holy Spirit, that all adds up to victory."

"Thank you for reminding me that all I need to do is receive my emotional healing the way I accepted Christ into my life. It is what He did for me on the cross, and not what I can do to obtain my healing."

"Old memories die hard, but your strength is in the Cross of Christ. I have to go. Oh, one more thing, why don't you get into something you like to take your mind off what happened to you. Oh, Mary Bell you are doing a great job with your Prayer, and Encouragement Group." Gotta go."

Clad in their black, broad brimmed hats, long black capes pants and shirts, Thor, Sam, and Cherry were ready. Cherry clutching Gideon in her arms, Thor ordered, "Anti Scanning shields on, Cathy activate the Retrieval Computer to send us on our way."

Seconds later, a blinding flash of blue light the 4 found themselves looking at countless numbers of leafless, light grey trees, in barren black humus soil. Thor stated, "I present to you the Dead Forest."

Sam inquired, "Do you have a map so we're not wondering around aimlessly?"

"The women should be in the center of the forest where the green sludge oasis is."

Cherry started at her husband and asked, "You know this because?"

"Because it is the only logical places they could be. Besides I had Cathy do a scan of the area earlier. Now let's get moving before it gets too late."

Cherry looked up at the evening sky and muttered, "The trouble with going to another world, the time is always different, and one suffers from Planet Lag."

"Okay we'll camp here tonight, it gonna be dark in about an hour or so anyways." ordered Thor.

Just as Sam made the fire, Patrick walked up to Thor and grumbled, "If you don't want Firefly and me around just say so and we'll go elsewhere."

Thor stared at the leprechaun and questioned, "What in the world are you babbling about?"

"You went off on another high priority mission left your two most valuable members of the team behind."

"And who are they pray tell?"

"That's it! We are out of here!" screamed Patrick.

Cherry inquired, "Did you fill out and send back the form Thor sent you?"

"Form? What form?"

"The form that tells says you are part of the first response team and where you can be reached."

Patrick smiled sheepishly then whispered, "Oh that form. It's around me home somewhere."

Pixy opened her backpack, took out a large thermos full of hot coffee, and foot-long hot sausage and pepper grinder, Italian, meat ball, Tuna and an Italian BMT. Then asked, "Okay, who wants what?"

Thor was washing down the last of his, Italian sub when he cocked his ear up and inquired, "Do you hear that? It sounds like someone screaming."

Cherry, Sam and the others looked up and saw a female sprite screaming, "Out of my way! Sprite coming in for an emergency landing!"

Right behind the sprite was a one manned spacecraft shaped like a bullet, with the wings shaped like triangles that came to a point in the back and a bubble on top, trying to shoot down the sprite. Everyone jumped up simultaneously, leveled their rifles at the craft and fired, chasing it away. The sprite clad I a pink short set landed, then tumbled several times then lay motionless face down on the soft black ground.

"Cherry knelt down and asked, "Sassy? What are you doing here?"

The sprite sat up moaning, "First I need to know where here is?"

"You are in The Dead Forest, on the moon of the Dark planet.

"Ah, okay I'm on the moon of the planet Adinidiin, cool."

Thor asked, "I just have one question? How did I get here form the Institute?"

"That is the sixty-four thousand questioned, all I know I was relaxing on my back deck in my shorts and top to unwind from the day. I remember hearing a Sprite wings just before I was jabbed in my thigh with a needle."

Thor questioned, "Are you saying that one of the sprites at the Institute is involved with the Blue Scarlet attacks?"

"You better believe I am and it's a female Sprite too."

"How do you know this?"

Sassy stared at Thor and moaned, "Duh! She was wearing an expensive perfume called, Galaxy Mist."

Cherry inquired, "Do you know where she was taking you?"

"While I was stuffed in that tiny cargo compartment, behind the pilot's seat of that one mane spacecraft, I overheard her talk to someone called Woody and telling him to get rid of the 'The Dreaded Twelve' because she had a better barging chip, me."

"Sassy. Are you sure it's one of the sprites from the Institute and not from Sprite King Mex's township?"

"Yes Sir."

Cherry asked, "How did you escape?"

"As soon as she landed the craft by the green oasis, I made a mad dash for freedom then took flight. That's when she took off after me."

Sam interjected, "It is possible that a female sprite could have a small one manned spacecraft hidden in the jungle just out of scanning range."

Patrick suggested, "Thor, I think we should break came and try and save those women no matter how wicked they are."

You are so right, Pat, alright everyone look alive it's time we got a move on."

"A Boss. My name is Patrick. Not Patty or Pat."

Thor ordered, "Pixy, and Sassy, fly a few feet ahead of us and warn us of anything suspicious."

No sooner the sprites soared skywards they shouted, "Hit the dirt!" and let themselves drop to the ground like a rock, as a one manned craft flew low overhead firing its energy weapons. Thor hollered, "Take cover!" Sam, Cherry, and Thor returned fire but missed as the craft swiftly soared away. Patrick stood up, swiftly rubbed his hands together and waited for the craft to make another attack. Then at just the right distance, the leprechaun quickly streaked hands out in front of him and sent a charge of electricity that slammed into the one manned craft. Sending it spiraling to the ground.

At the sight of the downed craft, Sam reached in the cockpit, picked up a small woman's shawl and said, "This must belong to one of the female sprites at the Institute and since there is no one in the pilot's seat, she has to be nearby."

An energy blast suddenly struck the downed craft Thor's quick reflexes kicked in, spun around, and returned fire then heard someone scream. Thor pointed in the direction of the Green Oasis and said, "We need to make tracks that way and fast Sam you take point. Pixy, Sassy, keep a bird's eye view on things."

An hour later, Sam put up his hand to signal everyone to halt and whispered, "The Green Oasis is just a head Pixy, Sassy, go see what you can find. The rest, look alive and be ready for anything."

CHAPTER 17

The Attack on Arrgua

Inside the oasis some fifty yards across, was crowded with lush trees, vines, and plenty of undergrowth. Thor stared at a mutilated body of Montronian woman and ordered, "Spread out and see if you can find the others."

Cherry hollered, "I found one over here! Or most of her anyways."

Patrick shouted, "There are two more bodies over here!"

Fourteen minutes later, eleven Montronian women lay dead on the ground Thor shook his head and said, "By the looks of things they were just a cat's paw in this whole thing."

Cherry stared at the Montroinan women with flesh tone skin, long triangle shaped head, long ears, bulging eyes, a long nose and said, "Now that is what I call ugly. No wonder they want to become human."

Just then, a Montronian woman crawled out from under a bush, with one leg hacked off and a deep gash in her side, pleading for help.

Patrick patched up the alien woman and asked, "How come you didn't bleed to death?"

"I found some moss that is great for clotting blood."

"Who did this to you and your friends?" questioned Patrick.

"A human by the name of Woody. But he was only following orders from an imp, who was watching from the shadows."

Thor took out his ruby pin, pointed it at the woman and said, "I am going to send you back to Montros, so you can be treated."

"Wait!" shouted the woman, "I have just one question. Why did he do this to me and my friends? We were told that if we allowed ourselves to be transformed into human women there would be adventure and excitement with lots of money. Why did he lie to us when all we wanted was to have a little fun?"

Thor sighed, wrote something on a slip of paper, gave it to the woman and said, "Give this to the one who will help you. He'll know what to do. I am the Alien Ambassador to Montros."

"I am called Sherry and thank you Human." Sherry glared at Cherry and stated, "Ugly? Are you calling me ugly, human? I won the Miss Montros Beauty Pageant 5 years in a row for your information." Sherry glanced at Thor and said, "You want to get me out of here before I barf. That human female is nauseating."

Thor sent her back to Montros, then, touched his watch and said, "Rock. Put out an All-Points Bulletin on Woody and is to be handled with extreme caution. Shoot to kill if he resists."

"Yes Sir."

Thor sent the remains of the dead women back to Montros for burial then asked, "Sam can I see that shawl you found in the downed draft? I have an idea."

Thor examined the cloak found a hair facial, walked to the pool of green sludge, and dropped it in. then stated, "If I miss my guess, that green goo will reproduce an exact copy of whoever was in that one manned space craft."

A few days later, Thor and the rest stared in unbelief, at the replica of Constance sitting on the edge of the in pool of sludge. Cherry asked, "Sprite Constance is responsible for all the Blue Scarlet attacks? I can't believe she is the master mine, there has to be another reason."

Thor stated, "Our next plan is to link Constance to the attacks before we jump to any conclusions. But for right now I think we should store the replica of Constance with Queen Diane and her husband."

Pixy spoke up, "I think the first thing we need to do is put some clothes on Constance's replica. The last thing she need is for everyone to see her bare sit-down."

"You ladies, take care of Constance's naked replica, while Sam, Patrick and I plan our next move."

Just then, Thor's computer watch rang, and a frantic voice on the other end hollered, "Galaxy Sentinel, we need you on Kylee right away! Then there was a scream and dead air."

Thor ordered, "Wrap up the dummy of Constance to take her with us, to the planet Kylee!" Thor touched his watch and said, "Cathy. Prepare to sling shot us to Kylee." Thor then announced, "Hold on everyone this is going to be a bumpy one."

A pale blue light suddenly enclosed everyone and sent them hurtling to Kylee tumbling on the grassland for ten yards before stopping. Cherry stood up and moaned, "Do me a favor Thor. When this is all over, delete the Sling Shot program."

"It's has to stay because it is part of the Retrieval Computer Program. But I'll ask Cathy if she can upgrade it."

Sam inquired, "Did you get a location of that caller?"

"No." Thor touched his computer watch and asked, "Computer. Can you give me the location of that last call?"

"The location is ten miles west of here."

Thor touched his watch and said, "Cathy. I need you to transport us ten miles west of our location."

"Yes sir. That will put you in the middle of the city of Arrgua."

"Tell Miss Puckett to have her teams ready for a Blue Scarlet attack on Kylee. Thor out."

In seconds, Thor and the group was thrown into the middle of the city. Thor sprang to his feet and shouted, "Miss Puckett! Arrgua is under attack by a huge cloud of Blue Scarlet! Get your men here, NOW!" Thor took out a blue crystal and said, "Ab. Arrgua is under attack by the cystic blue cloud. Tell me you have backup."

"My men will be there in a jiffy."

Cherry touched her husband's right arm saying, "Hon. That blue cloud is getting mighty close, we'd better head for cover."

Sassy pointed to a tall building and asked, "Isn't that Woody up there with something in his hands?"

"Sure is," answered Pixy, "Stand back guys, I'm on it." Pixy reared back and let go a loud will-o`-the-wisp war cry sounding more like an animal then a sprite. Transformed into a seven-foot fierce Wisp, took fight, and snatched Woody from the rooftop, hovered just in front of the blue cloud and said, "Give me a reason why I shouldn't let you suffer the fate you condemned so many innocent men women and children."

"I didn't do this! Honest! I heard about the attack and came to see if I could lend a hand."

"Tell me another one." Pixy flew back to Thor, placed Woody on the ground in front of him and inquired, "What shall we do with him, Sir?"

Woody stared at the reproduction of Constance, thought she was real and became extremely nervous and said, "Constance, ah what are you doing here?"

Cherry quickly replied, "She is speechless over the attack on this city."

Thor glared at Woody and stated, "I have a witness that will testify that you were the one who hacked up those women."

"I have no idea what you are talking about, I have proof that I was here in this city helping the poor and needy."

"Yeah, right Woody tell me another one. The next thing you're gonna try and sell some prime beach property in the middle of the desert. Get out of here before I throw you in front of that truck." Thor turned to Sam and the rest and said, "It's time to earn our pay for the month. Find a cleanup crew and join in."

Thor glanced up, saw Ab's aircraft spraying the cloud with grey spores trying keep the cloud from advancing. Thor looked down at Sassy hiding behind him and Said, "Don't worry, the cloud won't reach us."

With the blue cloud dispersed, Thor touched his computer watch and said, "I want all available personnel with strong stomachs to report to my location to aside in the clean up after a Blue Scarlet attack."

Hours later the cleanup was complete, Thor ordered everyone back to the Institute for rest. Then asked his wife, "Cherry, you wanna go for a cup of coffee at the Galaxy Cafe?"

"Sure, why not."

At the cafe, Thor set in a booth with his wife and saw Misty walking in with her boyfriend. She spotted Thor, approached him, and asked, "Would you like the report now or in the morning, Sir?"

"It's alright if you drop it off at my desk in the morning."

"Thanks Sir." Misty grabbed a cup of tea and walked to her house with Joe. Inside Misty put the Tram report on the counter so she would not forget to bring it to Thor in the morning.

Joe made a fire in the fire place, put on some soft music, removed his shoes and shirt, and had his hands on his belt buckle, when Misty asked, "What are you doing?"

"I thought we'd relax the way we did last week."

Misty frowned at her boyfriend and inquired, "After our talk with Rose and those dating classes on moral values, you still want to get into it?"

"That is their opinion about dating. I have my own ideas what we should do. Now let's go for it."

"We are not going to mess around this afternoon nor any other day Joe. I love you but, I will not lie to Cherry."

A puzzled Joe questioned, "Why the change? You were willing to fool around with me with last week."

"I think you look great Joe, but the price of sex, means moral degradation and I do not want to pay that price. Plus, I was naïve at the time."

"And?" questioned Joe with a smile on his face.

"Put your shirt and shoes back on and I'll serve us some pastry on the back patio."

Joe face turned red with anger and growled, "I see how it is. You have a double standard. You can crawl in bed with Todd, but not with me!"

Misty screamed, "Todd had a knife to my throat and was gonna kill me! Or don't you care that he could have slit my throat?"

"So, you say. Stop wasting time and come over here." replied Joe letting his pants drop to the floor.

Misty put on a pleasant smile, walked up to Joe, glanced down then asked, "Can you bend over?"

Joe happily did what Misty asked and inquired, "Okay now what?"

While Joe was bent over, Misty reached between his legs, grabbed his hand, and marched him outside, then threw his clothes in his face.

Joe quickly turned around and smiled sheepishly as three young women passed by. A short time later, the sprite security arrested Joe for indecent exposure.

Misty went out on her back patio with a cup of tea and prayed, "Lord, Joe looks real cute and it was hard for me to say no to him today, but I have to stop seeing him because I am afraid I will say yes to him next time."

Misty slipped into a pale green nightshirt, went into the bedroom, stared at her bed and was afraid that Todd might attack her again. She called Sassy and asked, "Hey Kiddo. Can you come over and keep me company for a few nights?"

"Scared you might wake up with some man in bed with you holding a knife to your throat?"

"You know it."

"Be there in a jiff."

That night in her dark bedroom, Misty felt someone behind her in bed while she slept and was afraid to move. She then muttered, "Joe, get out of my bed right now or so help me it will be the last thing you ever do." Misty rolled on her back to see who it was. Suddenly, a distorted figure landed on top of her sending her thrashing about as she screamed, "Get off me! Get off me! Get off me!"

Sassy charged in the room, put on the overhead light, grabbed Misty saying, "Calm down. No one is attacking you."

"Then who the blazes was on top of me trying to kill me!"

Sassy picked up a large tattered rabbit and said, "Your huge stuffed bunny fell off the shelf above your bed."

"I need a cup of hot Chamomile tea to settle my nerves. Then I'm going to put Mr. Rabbit on the couch in the living room."

The next morning, Misty dawn her bathrobe, walked in the kitchen and asked, "Sassy, what would you like to eat?"

Sassy snickered, "Any more vicious stuffed animals attack you last night?"

"Ha, ha very funny. What do you want for your morning meat?"

"How about an oatmeal and sardine omelet?"

"Gross. How can you eat all that weird stuff? What if I give you a ham and cheese omelet with home fries with toast and jam?"

"Okay, that will work. Oh hey. Mary Bell's Prayer and encouragement group is tonight. I think you should attend. You never know when you're gonna be attacked by a savage bloodthirsty bunny."

"Will you stop it already? And yes, I will go to the meeting."

Sassy took a bite of her egg and reported, "Oh. Keep your eye on Constance, she may be the one behind the Blue Scarlet attacks."

"Hey gotta go drop off my report to Thor this morning. Coming?"

"Be there in jiff. Oh hey. One more thing. I see you are doing it on a regular basis with Joe. When Thor finds out he is going to kick you out of the Institute for good."

A puzzled Missy inquired, "What are you talking about? I lost control with Joe once and that's all."

Missy held a three inch in diameter silver ball with six octagonal blue crystals and stated, "This tells me otherwise."

"What in the world is that, pray tell?"

"Guys use it to make women sprites more acceptable for intimacy."

"What?" Screamed Missy. Her eyes narrowed and growled, "That has to be Joe's and he must have used it last week to get me to mess around with him. Give it to me. I am going to ram it down his throat! For using that on me. Than I am going to report him to Thor. Now let's go before I am late."

Sassy hopped in her electric cart with Misty and hollered, "To the Institute and don't spare the horses!"

On their way to the Institute, Sassy spotted Constance and exclaimed, "Good Lord girl you look like crap. What did you do fly into a tree?"

"Something like that."

"Why aren't you taking the tram?" questioned Misty.

"It's too nice of a day to be underground." Sassy helped Constance in the cart and sped off.

At the Institute, Missy gave Lacy the report then handed her the silver ball with six octagonal blue crystals and stated, "Give this to Thor and tell him that Joe was using it on me."

Constance entered Thor's outer office and asked, "Lacy, is Thor in? He wants to see me about something."

"Go right in."

Constance walked in, then stopped abruptly and stared the plant reproduction of herself sitting on top of the desk. Then stated, "If that is supposed to be me. She is a poor reproduction, I am not that fat, and my hair is not that dark."

Thor sitting behind his desk, tapped the intercom, and said, "You can come in now Cherry." Thor glared at Constance and ordered, "Sit. Cherry and I have a few questions and you better have the right answers, or your butt is going to be in a sling. Young Lady."

"I don't know what you are talking about. I've done nothing wrong."

"I suppose you don't know a Woody P. Juarez, the X-manager of the Cave Jumpers who also helped create the Nightwalker monster that Terrorized the Alliance?"

"No sir I don't."

"I think you do. Because you two have been seen together murdering 12 women."

"I think I bumped into the guy once or twice but that's all."

"Then tell me how did your hair get in the cockpit of the one-man space craft that tried to kill Sassy, Sam, Cherry and me?"

"A hair Sir? How do you know it's mine?"

"Because it was dropped in the green goo and it reproduced an exact copy of you. Care to explain that one?"

"I never left this planetoid and I think someone is trying to set me up as the monster that's been releasing the Blue Scarlet Gas."

"There is a lot of evidence stacked against you Miss Constance and your answers are pretty weak."

"If you don't mind me asking, Sir what do you have against me?"

Cherry examined the sprite's injuries and asked, "How did you get so banged up?"

"I fell if it's any business of yours."

Cherry growled, "Keep a civil tongue in your mouth Miss Constance, if you don't want to go on report. All I am saying is, your injuries are conducive to a crash landing in a one manned spacecraft."

Thor stated, "From here on in you are to report to your boss, Misty every morning before you go work, then check in with her every evening before you go home. Is that clear Miss Constance?

"What? You have to be kidding me!"

"Lower your voice or I'll throw you in a cell room right now! You are dismissed Miss Constance."

After the sprite left, Cherry turned to Thor and said, "She is hiding something."

"We have to keep an eye on her, she is up to something no good. It maybe another prank, but we'll have to keep her under close scrutiny."

CHAPTER 18

Too Close to Home

Fare Thor's, disabled Will-o`-the -wisp daughter approached him in her hover chair threw a photo of him and Rose on his desk and screamed, "How could you Dad?"

Thor looked at Fara in her tear stained eyes and inquired, "You wanna tell me what's bothering you?"

"You cheated on Mom!"|

"If you look close enough you will see that's not me and Rose and that is not the hot springs."

Fara studied the photo and said, "Son of a gun, you are right. Dad." she gave Thor a hug and apologized for doubting him.

Thor stated, "I am trying to find out who is behind these photos you want to go to the cafe for a cup of coffee and chat a while?"

"Sure."

As Thor opened his office door Horatio, the royal blue, Macaw, flew in, landed on Thor's shoulder, and said, "I did my normal scan of the area, and there is something you ought to see."

Thor followed Horatio with Cherry and Fare to Constance's backyard, and notice how the rows in the garden were neatly raised up and cultivated? The bird stated, "If you dig up the end of the row you will find something interesting."

Thor took the nearby shovel, stuck it in the ground, Constance raced out the sliding glass door of her home screaming, "Thief! Thief! Get out of my garden!"

The bird extended his talons and attacked Constance giving Thor the time he needed. The shovel struck something wooden under the dirt. Cherry quickly knelt, brushed away the soil and found a covered wooden trough filled with grapefruit sized Blue Scarlet spheres. Thor shouted, "Cherry grab Constance!"

Cherry took hold of Constance, and held the sprite in a full-nelson as Thor carefully picked up a sphere from the trough and asked, "Do you have a good explanation for this?"

Thor touched his watch and said, "Rock, have your men suit up in hazmat gear and meet me in Constance's back yard. She has I don't know how many dozens of Blue Scarlet spheres burred in her garden." Thor then contacted Moonbeam and said, "Have your men clear the housing project for several blocks around Constance's place. Horatio found a stash of orbs buried in her back yard."

Back in Thor's office with Constance's in chains, he proceeded to interrogate her, but she remained silent. Thor looked at his wife and said, "See what you can get out of her."

After an hour, more of fierce questioning, Thor took his broad sword, walked up to Constance, and said, "No more stalling. Tell me why there are over three dozen Blue Scarlet orbs buried in your garden or I will cut you in half."

"Aren't you carrying things a bit too far Thor?" questioned Cherry.

"I know what I am doing so stay out of this."

"Hacking up a suspect is going way overboard, now back off, Hon."

Thor took a firm grip on his broad sword and buried in Constance's side, blood poured out of her wound, she went into convulsions and fell to the floor stiff. Cherry stared at her husband in horror that he would do such a horrible thing. Thor knelt, opened Constance's blouse, peeled back the artificial skin, and showed Cherry the metallic frame of an android.

Cherry inquired, "Where is the real Constance if she's not the master mind?"

Thor touched his watch and said, "Teeny, I need to see you in my office pronto and bring your tools with you."

Fifteen minutes later Teeny walked in, saw sprite Constance on the floor and exclaimed, "A mandroid, how about that."

Thor stated, "Don't you mean android?"

"No, it is a mandroid. A robot that breaths, bleeds and has emotions like a normal human. I hope you didn't destroy it. Oh, Amanda is back together and is working just fine. I removed the triggering device and destroyed it."

Amanda walked in smiled sweetly at Thor and said, "Thank you for rescuing me." Stared at Constance on the floor and said, "The poor thing." then stated, "Thor, Sir, Teeny says I have a job working for Mike and Company acting group. Oh Teeny, Cindy said she is going to shut down for two days to do a complete diagnostic on all her systems."

Thor asked Teeny as he removed the Constance's head, "Can you tell me how long she's been active and where did she come from?"

"Reading the data file who knows if there was a real sprite Constance. She was designed to be the fall guy for the attacks that's been going on here of lately. Oh, the android Stella, she is history. She was too badly damaged to repair. Give me a hand putting Constance in the cart, so I can bring her to my workshop."

"I think there is a real sprite Constance somewhere because I have a replica of her. Can you repair her then give her a new personality" asked Thor.

"You don't want much. But I think I can do it. All you did was sever a few wires. When I am finished with her she will remember her friends but not her past."

"Don't make her obnoxiously nice."

"I will also download all information from Constance's memory bank and give it to you. Now if you will excuse me I have a mandroid to fix."

Thor touched his computer watch and said, "Belinda, I want you and Fara to go through Constance's home with a fine-tooth comb and see what you can come up with in the way of evidence that will prove she was more than a robot."

"You've got it dad."

Moonbeam brought Sprite Joe in Thor's office with a blanket wrapped around him and stated, "Joe was arrested in front of Misty's home in his altogether."

Thanks, I'll take it from here. Thor stared at Joe and inquired, "You want to explain why you were outside without a stitch of clothes on?"

"It's all Misty's fault."

Thor touched his computer watch and said, "Misty, will you report to my office right away."

A minutes later, Misty walked in, saw Joe, and moaned. "Oh. I suppose you want to talk to me about why I tossed Joe out on his butt. It was the only way I could think of keeping him from getting fresh with me."

Thor stared at Joe and asked, "Were you trying to convince Misty to get in bed with you?"

Joe hung his head, ashamed of his actions and answered, "Yes, Sir. I was."

"You need to develop a relationship based on trust and respect. Then, after the wedding you get to enjoy the fruit of your labor with your wife. If you base your relationship on sex, it will go sour on you sooner or later. So, slow down and treat Misty nice, or you will have me to deal with."

"Can I have my clothes back Sir."

"Sure, see the one who arrested you for them."

After Joe left, Thor asked Misty, "Sit on my desk, so I can talk to you."

Misty hopped up on Thor's desk and stared into his eyes expecting to have her ears pinned back for what she did with Joe. Instead, Thor smiled and stated, "I am proud of the way you handled yourself by not giving into temptation with Joe."

"But I," Thor stopped Misty and said, "You didn't the second time. Forgiveness is in the cross of Christ. Repent of your sin and go on and stop feeling guilty."

"Yes Sir."

Cherry walked in Thor's office, thought about the Mandroid Constance and Inquired, "Hon. The hair on that robot Constance. What do you suppose would have happened if we dropped hair follicles in that green goo?"

"Nothing. It wouldn't have the DNA to reproduce anything. I think."

Thor touched his watch and asked, "Teeny, the hair on that Mandroid. Is it human hair or is it artificial?"

"There is no question about, that it's artificial."

"Thanks." Thor gazed at his wife reported, "The hair on the robot is artificial. Which means the real Constance is in hiding hoping we won't find her decoy."

Cherry pointed to the plant reproduction of Constance and asked, "What do we do with her?"

"Have one of the woman put a bathing suit on her, then position her on top of the falls in the Arboretum."

"How about if we make a few more plant reproductions and place them in that grassy spot on the right side of the Botanical garden."

"Sounds like a plan. Let's go for it." Then she contacted Cathy and told her what the plan was.

Cherry put her arms around Thor's neck and asked, "Weren't we going to the Galaxy Cafe for coffee before we were so rudely interrupted?"

Thor and Cherry were on their way out the office door when Cathy caught them and inquired, "Where is the plant reproduction?"

Thor told His wife, "Go on ahead. I'll meet you there in a few minutes." Thor closed the office door and gave Cathy a secret project to work on.

At the cafe, Thor spent a good part of two hours with his wife talking and fellowshipping with friends. On their way home late, that evening they decided to walk. Halfway down the path from the housing project to the Institute, Thor stopped and said, "Cherry, listen. That sounds like Misty crying. You wait here, while I go see."

"Oh, no you don't I'm right behind you."

Thor carefully walked through the dark jungle and up behind Misty. She let out a scream, jumped to her feet and tried to fly away. Thor quickly grabbed her foot, but Misty kept screaming, "Don't kill me! I won't tell honest I won't!" kicking and screaming in terror. Cherry walked up to the sprite and stated, "Relax Misty. It's just Thor and me."

Cherry comforted the trouble sprite and asked, "Who is out to kill you?"

Misty showed Thor the letter she received in the mail he examined the envelop and said, "Fancy letter." then read the letter that said, "If you say one word to anyone about who I am I will make sure you die slowly."

Thor inquired, "Do you know who the person is that sent you this letter?"

"No Sir."

"Think. Did you hear Todd say anything when he forced you in bed with him at knife point?"

"Just a lot of babbling nonsense. Wait, when you made me chief honcho, I took some pictures of each Tram Depot."

Thor directed, "Cherry, you take Misty to her place and go through those pictures, I want to compare Constance's stationary to this letter."

As Thor got up to go, Cherry touched his arm and inquired, "Do you think we should check: Mimi, Darlene and Susanna to make sure they are not mandroids? After all those three chummed around with Constance."

"Excellent idea. Contact Doc Chrissy and have her do an exam on those three sprites right away."

In Misty's home, Cherry and Misty carefully went over the photos until they came to one picture of Woody in the Beach Tram Dept. giving Constance a large package. Cherry commented, "I bet the mandroid is in that package. Hold onto that picture." Cherry touched her computer watch and said, "Misty and I are going to the Beach Tram Depot to check on a lead. Meet us there."

At the Beach Depot, Cherry climbed in the rubbish bin and searched through all kinds of wrappers and boxes. She then shouted,

"Bingo!" and passed a crate to Misty, three feet tall, by two-foot square, she touched her watch and said, "Teeny. Get your scrawny little butt to the Beach Tram Depot, Now!"

"Can't it wait? I am in the middle of something important at the moment."

"Put your lady friend on hold and get here now!"

Ten minutes later, Teeny sauntered in the depot with Thor and bellowed, "What is it that you want?"

Cherry showed Teeny the box and asked, "Well, what do you think?"

"You called me down her just to show me a box?"

"Could someone have shipped a mandroid in it?"

"Not only could, they but they did. Be right back." Teeny leaped in the dumpster, dove under the trash, then pushed out a large soft foam form, put it in the crate and said, "The Mandroid Constance was in packaged in this. Misty your Constance's size, step in the box for a minute." Then said, "You see, the form fits Misty like a glove."

Cherry showed Thor the photo; he glanced at the box then at the picture and said, "Yup, the box in the picture matches the one we have. Not only that, the stationary I found in Constance's home matches the letter Misty received right down to the hand writing. What I want to know is how Woody got that mandroid on this planetoid without anyone knowing it." Thor put his arm around Cherry and said, "I'll have the lab go over the crate, maybe they can come up with some more evidence. Thor turned to Misty and asked, "Where were you when you took this picture?"

"On the end of the platform looking this way."

Thor stood where Misty took the photo, looked through the large picture window into the Tram office. Walked in the office, searched Constance's desk for a portal remote, looked up and stared at the blank wall, walked up to it, and rubbed his hand on the wall. He then shouted, "Teeny, bring that mandroid of Constance in here."

Fourteen minutes later, Teeny escorted the sprite robot in the office and asked, "Now what?"

The mandroid walked to the wall, placed both hands on it and opened a portal. Thor grabbed the mandroid before it could enter, stepped through for a moment and muttered, "This in the 'Face Master's office." Then returned to the Tram Station and asked, "Teeny is there any way we can shut this wall portal down permanently?"

"All you have to do is shoot the controls in that fancy ceiling molding. Here you can use my energy pistol."

Once the wall portal was destroyed Thor asked, "Teeny, how are you coming with Constance's new personality?"

"Give me a day another day and I'll have all the kinks worked out of it."

"I need her ready to go within the hour."

"You've got it, Boss."

Thor touched his computer watch and said, "Subspace operator, connect me to the Planet Montros. I want to speak to the one in charge of the military."

"That would be the First Selectman. I'll connect you."

A deep voice answered, "This is First Selectman, Ammihud Pedahzur can I help you."

"This Thor, the Alien Ambassador to Montros, I need two hundred of your men to surround a freestanding gray stone building in the middle of a field of tall green grass just outside of the city of Batra. One of the people responsible for the Blue Scarlet attacks is hiding in that building."

"Can you give me an address?"

"141 Winding Way. Batra, planet Montros"

"You've got it."

Cherry walked in the infirmary thirty minutes later, found; Mimi, Darlene and Susanna sitting on exam tables clad in Johnny-coats looking scared. Mimi asked, "Cherry. Are we going to shrivel up and die like Christy said? I don't want to look like a prune."

"I'll check. It maybe it's a computer glitch."

Cherry approached the doctor and asked, "Well are they sprites or mandroid?"

"I have one more test to perform then I'll know."

Christy had Mimi get on the exam table, lay on her stomach, and said to her, "This may sting a bit." The Doctor slowly inserted a needle in Mimi's right butt cheek four inches and said, "If Mimi was a mandroid I would not be able to shove the needle in her keister this far for a DNA sample."

Ten minutes later, Mimi, Darlene and Susanna walked out of the infirmary with sore bottoms. Cherry caught up to them and said, "Just before I leave for Montros, I'll buy the three of you Spicy Curly fries and burgers."

"How about a pillow to go with that?" questioned Susanna.

CHAPTER 19

The hunt

Hunkered down behind some boulders on the planet Montros, the Montronian commander turned to Thor and inquired, "How many are holding up inside?"

"One dangerous 35-inch sprite that looks just like this mandroid."

"You have got to be kidding me? You called me out here with two hundred heavily armed men to capture a female sprite? I'm calling this idiotic attack off right now."

"I wouldn't do that Sir."

As the commander's men rose to leave, blasts from an automatic energy rifle took out 50 of his men. Thor hollered, "Constance! Lay down your weapon and surrender. You have nowhere to run!"

Cherry then bellowed, "Constance, it's me Cherry. Please lay down your weapon and surrender before you get hurt!"

A long, high pitched bloodcurdling screech split the afternoon sky. The Commander stated, "That was no sprite. You want to level with me and tell me just what we are dealing with?"

"After hearing that scream, I have no idea what is inside at this moment."

A three foot tall dark gray figure with horns and wings like bat appeared in the window for a brief moment. Thor stared at the ghastly shape and stated, "That's a Banshee."

The commander asked, "Now will you let me do things my way?"

"Go ahead. But I don't think your show of force will do any good."

Seconds later, the building was hit with thousands blast energy from all sides that perforated the building. Thirteen minutes later the Commander called a cease fire, turned to Thor, and said, "No one could have lived through that barrage."

"Let's wait and see." Thor peeked over the top of the rock and saw the Banshee pointing an energy rifle at him. He pulled his head down just as a blast of energy ricocheted off the boulder and said, "You were saying Commander."

Thor picked up a one-foot long branch that was 2 inches think and asked, "Commander, May I see your knife?"

Thor sharpened one end, gave it to the Mandroid Constance saying, "Your framework will withstand the blast of energy from her rifle. I want you to kill that thing with this."

Constance, put that pointed shaft of wood down the back of her slacks, slowly walked towards the building and hollered, "Hey, Bean-shìdh, I have a gift for you."

"My name real name is Annwn, I just took the form of the real Constance to throw people off. Now, what do you want robot?"

"Ah yes Annwn, a mythical name in the other world. Why did you change your appearance?"

"I grew tired of hiding who I was. Don't come any closer, robot or I will blast you into millions of pieces."

"All I wanted to do is give you something you deserve."

Let go a shriek and fired a blast of energy at Constance just missing her head. Constance stated, "You are either a poor shot, or there is still some feeling inside of you and you don't want to take a life."

"Shut up!" shouted Annwn, and fired another wild shot at Constance.

The mandroid commented, "Isn't a Bean-shìdh an Irish Myth about a female sprite who wails when someone is going to die? So why are you going around killing people?"

"That's none of your businesses."

"Are you going to come outside so I can give you your gift? Or do I have to break down the door."

Annwn walked outside with her energy rifle in her hands and asked, "What is this so-called gift you want to give me?"

"This!" shouted Constance, knocked the gun from her hands, quickly reached behind her, grabbed the wooden spike, and shoved it in the banshee's chest as far as it would go, then grabbed her by the throat and squeezed.

Annwn shrieked and thrashed about trying to break free from the mandroid's vice like grip but couldn't.

With Constance's free hand, she removed the wooden shaft from Annwn's chest and drove it through Annwn face, killing her.

Thor walked up to Constance, patted her on the head and said, "Good work."

Constance started at the dead banshee, looked up at Thor and said, "I wish I didn't have to kill her."

The commander ordered, "Check the building! If it moves kill it. Then, set the explosive charges. I don't want to see one brink upon another!"

Thor glanced down again and Annwn's body was gone." and thought, "Maybe she is not dead."

The alien commander shook Thor's his hand and thanked him for his help and wished him good luck on finding on finding Woody. Thor turned to his wife and suggested, "What do you say we go to a White Forest Café on Avalon Prime, grab a cup of coffee and do some brainstorming there."

An hour later, sitting in a booth in the white Forest café Cherry took a swallow of her Coconut-hazelnut coffee and said, "I wonder where the real Constance is?" She looked at Thor and said, "Since Woody is a womanizer, I'll check with some of my lady contacts to see if they know where he is. While I am doing that, I'll take care of Constance and dress her up in something sleazy and see what you can find out with the local bar flies.

Constance stared at Cherry and questioned, "What if I don't want to wear something that says I have a low moral character? I have scruples even though I am mandroid."

Thor briskly rubbed his knuckles on top of Constance's head then stated, "I'll get Mike, of Mike and Company acting group to change your looks?"

"That'll work. And please no more nuggies it messes my hair up."

Cherry, call Mike and see if how soon he can get here for a makeup job for Conscience and me." Thor spotted a man and said, "If you will excuse me, I need to talk to that lowlife who just came in." Thor approached a tall young man in his twenties dressed in a t-shirt, jeans, and white running shoes. Pushed him in the booth and sat down preventing him from escaping and questioned, "Okay Jake. What's going down concerning Blue Scarlet?"

"Thor! I've been keeping myself clean so don't come around bothering me."

"You couldn't stay out of trouble if your life depended on it Jake. Now what have you heard concerning Blue Scarlet?"

"Nothing, honest."

"Let's take a walk to the men's room."

Thor locked the men's room door, shoved Jake in the handicapped stall, pushed his head in the toilet and flushed it. Then repeated the question.

"After the fourth time, Thor hauled Jake to his feet and asked, "What's going down concerning Blue Scarlet?" then stuck his energy pistol to Jake's head saying, "If you don't tell me, I am going to pull the trigger and give you one big whopper of a headache for a day."

"Alright, alright, Woody is going to have a meeting this evening at the Black Hole Bar on Deadwood Avenue. Now can I dry off and get back to my coffee?"

"Sure. But, not with this." and took a packet of yellow powder out of Jake's pocket and flushed it down the toilet.

Jake took two steps, Thor grabbed him by the back of his collar and stated, "Pastor Joshua has been asking for you. I want to see you in church on Sundays all cleaned up." Then gave him a slight shove.

Thor stepped out of the men's room, greeted Mike and his wife Heather, and said, "Thank you for coming on such a short notice, but do you think you can do a quick make over for Constance and me?"

My van is in the parking lot."

Ten minutes later, Mike gave Constance a cute button nose, changed the shape of her ears and augmented her figure, Heather helped Conscience out in a thin, low cut dress that stopped just below her knees. Mike then gave Thor a new face and long hair. Thor thanked Mike and kissed Cherry and said, "I'll meet you in the Grecian Diner at nine o'clock."

Walking up to the 'Black Hole Bar, Conscience looked up at Thor and inquired, "Sir, what do you want me to do if some guy grabbed my posterior?"

"Break his arm." Thor opened the door to the bar, and walked in a dark, smoky room filled with the dregs of the galaxy. Conscience sat on a bar stool, crossed her legs, and ordered a long neck. A short man in his fifties, clad in a wrinkled suit and a five o'clock shadow sat on the Constance's right, place his hand on her thigh and asked, "How about you and I get to know each other better? What'd ya say?"

"Sir. Take your hand off my thigh before I break your arm."

"The drunk moved his hand further up Conscience's thigh and asked, "What's your price little lady?"

Constance seized his wrist, jerked it up and back throwing him off the bars tool. The drunk staggered to his feet hollering, "You broke my arm!"

"I'll break more than your arm if you don't leave me alone."

Conscience turned around, leaned forward and inquired, "Hey bar keep. My friend and I are looking for Woody."

"I don't know who you are talking about."

"Just tell him there is a woman who is looking for some action from him."

"Oh! That Woody! He is in the back room ready to start a meeting of some sort."

"Thanks."

"But, you're a sprite."

Yeah. So, what."

"Why are you hanging around a human?"

"A girl needs protection in my kind of work. Now if you will excuse me. My client awaits."

Constance sat on Thor's shoulder as he walked through the bar and into the back and opened the door. Thor slowly scanned the room filled with Montronian men disguised as humans and asked, "Getting ready for another attack?"

Woody stared at Thor and Conscience and stated, "This is a closed meeting."

Constance stood on Thor's shoulder and hollered, "Nobody move! This is a raid!" then sprang forward onto Woody. Thor grabbed a wooden chair and began to swing it around. Woody threw the sprite across the room against the wall. She jumped to her feet and let out a hideous screech, terrorizing everyone in the room. Thor ordered, "Alright you bunch of losers, stand against the back wall."

One inquired, "Or what? Murder us in cold blood?"

"No. I am the alien Ambassador to Montros and you gentlemen are going back." Thor took out his ruby pen and activated it. The men's bodies quickly turned a pale yellow for two seconds then vanished.

Constance, pointed to the door and asked, "Woody got away, but what are we going to do about those guys in the doorway?"

Thor glanced at Constance and suggested, "You take the big guys, I'll take the little ones."

"What?" hollered the Sprite, picking up a broken chair leg to defend herself.

Suddenly, the front door of the bar flew opened and a thunderous roar resounded through the place. The attackers turned with a start to see a huge male lion entering followed by a stout man with red hair. Sam stared at the mob and questioned, "Who wants to be kitten's first snack, please step forward."

A man in the mob, swung his energy pistil up and fired a short blast at the lion. The enormous cat bounded across the bar, sending men scattering everywhere, jumped on the one who fire at him, and let out a roar, then took the guy's head in his mouth. Thor hollered,

"General! Take that man's head out of your mouth! He could make you sick."

The lion did not pay attention to Thor but slowly closed his mouth on the man's. Head. Thor shouted, "General Heel!"

The cat dropped the thug, walked to Thor, sat, and growled. Sam stated, "Okay everyone back to drinking your swill. Sam hauled the man up by his collar and asked, "Buddy. Did you get kicked in the head when you were young? You do not take on a lion that stands five feet from front paw to ear tip. Unless you want to die."

"Go suck an egg pops."

"Be nice and answer my question or you are lion food." stated Thor, "Where is Woody?"

"I'm not going to tell you. So, feed me to that overgrown cat."

"Constance, walked up to the man, looked up at him and stated, "Kindly answer Sam's question or you'll feel pain the likes you never felt before."

"Get out of here Insect before I step on you."

Conscience, ripped opened the man's shirt, grabbed his flabby stomach, and muttered, "Activating pain generator."The man's body stiffened as he screamed in shier agony for a minute. Conscience let go of the man as he fell to the floor. She then questioned, "That was my low setting. Would you like to try for the highest? Now, where is Woody P. Juarez the x-manager of the Cave Jumpers?"

"Oh! That Woody! He likes to hang out on the planet Kylee. The jungle world that is still full of weird vicious animals and plant life that can strip the flesh off your bones in seconds."

Sam took a small spray container from his pocket, sprayed the man's face, and said, "That's so we know where to find you just in case you are lying."

The man glared at Constance and growled, "What are you looking at you little Creep?"

"Nothing." Constance belted him between his pockets, sending him on his knees groaning.

The sprite got in his face and stated, "That's for not being nice to me." she climbed on General's back and said, "Giddy up Kitty."

CHAPTER 20

Mandroid Constance

Sitting in the chrome, Grecian Diner with its many marble statues from Earth and a large, three-dimensional image of the Acropolis on one wall. A waitress walked up to the table, dressed in the traditional Greek clothing. Thor glanced at Sam and Conscience asked, "What would you 2 like?"

Sam put down his menu and said, "I'll have Moussaka, coffee and a tossed salad."

Constance smiled and said, "I'll have the same and so will Thor my best bud."

After the waitress left, Thor inquired, "Constance, you can eat food?"

"Oh sure, I prosses it into energy then vaporize the remains in my disposal chamber. Hey. Here come Cherry! Hi Mom!"

Cherry gave Thor a kiss, glanced at Conscience and whispered, "We have to talk later. Oh, I received a call from Rock and he told me to tell you that General arrived back at the Institute safe and sound. Oh hey, I want a Geek salad with mine."

Thor inquired, "Cherry. What have you learned from your connections?"

"Woody is a lady's man and has convinced twelve women from this planet to go with him somewhere."

"He's hiding out on the planet Kylee. I just pray Woody doesn't murder those women too."

Patrick and his sprite wife Pixy walked up, sat down and Patrick stated, "Rock informed me that there is trouble brewing and you might need our help."

"The more the merrier. We have to go to Kylee and get Woody. Are you two in?"

"Kylee? Ah, Sir O'Hara, the head of me people hasn't been able to restore the whole planet to its original pristine condition yet. There are still things roaming around outside of the Lost Valley that you do not want to tangle with."

"Are you with us or not?"

Patrick swallowed hard and said, "We're in aren't, we me Firefly."

Pixy glared Conscience and complained, "After all she did Sir. You're bringing her along."

"Pixie, meet Mandroid Constance."

"Shut up! She's an android. No way."

"Not an android a Mandroid it's a lot better."

Cherry inquired, "If we are going straight to the Kylee where are we going to get our supplies? You know tents, food, rain gear, food, those things you cut the underbrush with, food."

Thor rubbed his wife's shoulders and replied, "Don't worry Sweetheart, we will have plenty of food this trip. Won't we Patrick?"

Constance tapped Thor's shoulder and asked, "Can you buy me some jeans hiking boots and a blouse for this mission? I don't want to go tramping around a jungle in this flimsy dress."

Thor took a swallow of his coffee and said, "We are gonna have to go back to the Institute for Star Fire Two. Because we can't use a portal or the Retrieval Computer to get to Kylee."

Sam smiled and said, "Good. That will give me time to get my javelin."

Cherry glanced at Sam and said, "Can you tell Dora I have the yarn she has been wanting."

Thor stated, "The food is here so let's chow down and be on our way."

Back on the planetoid, Cherry sat on the front porch of her cottage by Smile Lake with her husband and asked, "Why is Conscience calling me Mom and you Dad? Did you adopt her too?"

"I have no idea. Maybe there is something inside that mandroid that is looking for some type of security."

Constance walked on the porch, sat in Cherry's lap, put her arms around her neck and asked, "Mom, can I stay here with you tonight?"

Cherry rested her head-on top of Conscience's head and said, "You can stay as long as you like. Why don't you go wash up I'll find you a nighty, and Thor will make up the couch for you tonight."

"That's alright, I can stand in a corner somewhere out of your way."

"Nonsense, you're my daughter and I am going to take good care of you. Do you want me to help you to wash up?"

"Could you mommy."

Cherry smiled as she kissed Thor and said, "I'll talk to you later. Our little girl needs some attention."

Teen walked on the porch drinking an iced tea, sat down, and inquired, "How's things going with the Mandroid Conscience?"

Thor glared at Teeny and stated, "Before I give your butt a good swift kick. Explain to me why a fancy robot is calling Cherry mom and me, dad and acting like an insecure little girl?"

"Come on Thor. You're pulling my leg. Mandroid don't act like that."

"Oh? Follow me and see for yourself."

Teeny walked in the cottage with Thor and saw Cherry sitting in a rocking-chair singing a lullaby to Conscience in her lap. Teeny's jaw hit the floor in shock, looked at Thor and shrugged his shoulders.

Cherry put Conscience on the couch, covered her over, smiled and said, "You guys are gonna have to leave, I don't want you to disturb our daughter."

The next morning, Teeny knocked on the door and inquired, "Cherry. Would you mind if I checked Conscience? I want to find out why she is acting strangely. A mandroid should not be acting like a human child."

Conscience walked in the room clad in her light blue baby doll Pjs and asked, you wanted to see me Teeny?"

"I would like to check your systems to make sure everything is running properly."

Constance turned around and lifted her long light brown hair off the back of her neck. Teeny opened a small door just below her skull, inserted a small white octagonal plug attached to a cord. Then plugged it into a thin, twelve by six-inch flat white plastic computer board. A colorful schematic of Constance's systems appeared on the board. Teeny carefully studied Constance's systems and stated, "Your artificial circulatory system is fine. Wait a minute, where did all those neural fibers come from? Constance I'm going to prick you somewhere you can't see and tell me if you feel anything."

"Ouch! That was more than a prick!"

Teeny disconnected Constance saying, "Cherry, you are the proud mother of the first artificial life form. Even though Constance is a mandroid, she has all the abilities and feelings of a human eight-year-old child."

"Yeah but she has the body of an adult female sprite in her twenties. Is there anything you can do to change that?"

Teeny pondered Cherry's question for a minute and sated, "If she doesn't put on any makeup, or put on a booby catcher, then put her hair up in pigtails, it just might do the trick. Hey, got to go, Cindy wants to go exploring today."

After Teeny left, Tippy came out of her room, gave Constance a hug saying, "Welcome to the family, little sis. Mom I know where I can put my hands on some cream that will shrink her boobs down to match her age." Tippy stared at her mother and asked, "Do you know where you are going to put her?"

"Haven't a clue just yet."

"She can stay with me in my room." stated Tippy.

"As long as you don't mind. It is alright with me."

Heather opened the screen door poked her head in and asked, "Mike told me somebody here called for a Mandroid Makeover." She then walked in, studied Constance figure and said, "I can see why you want her looking younger. She has the mind of an eight-year-old and the body of someone in their twenties."

"How much is this gonna cost me?" questioned Cherry.

"One afternoon on your gorgeous beach will be more than enough payment."

Tippy instructed, "Constance, go in my room, take off your clothes and put on my night shirt. We'll be in, in a few minutes." Tippy glared at Heather and inquired, "Are you sure you can do it without making her look like a freak?"

"I'll let you watch. If it is not to your liking, I'll change her back before it becomes permanent."

Two hours later, Constance walked out of the room escorted by Tippy, clad in pink underwear and a t-shirt and asked, "What do you think mom?"

"Perfect. Now put some clothes on her."

Thor gave his wife a kiss on her lips and asked, "Where is your stuff? We're almost ready to go to Kylee."

"I am not going with you this time. I have to take care of Constance."

"By the way, where is she?"

"Right here." stated Constance,"

"There's my little girl." stated Thor. "Why don't you go outside and play on the beach."

Conscience dashed outside slamming the screen door behind her. Thor turned to Heather and said, "Thank you. She looks her age now. What do I owe you?"

"Just some time on your beach will do. Will you excuse me? I have to put on my bathing suit."

Thor stepped outside on the front porch to watch his new daughter play in the sand. Looked up and saw Mary Bell flying right towards him, hollering, "In coming sprite!" and plowed into Thor knocking him off his feet. Mary Bell stood up all excited and inquired, "I just heard you have a new daughter. Where is she, where, where, where?"

Thor rose to his feet and asked, "Are you alright Mrs. Bell? Oh, and that's our new daughter over there playing in the sand."

Mary Bell squinted her eyes at the diminutive mandroid and asked, "Who made Constance look so young?"

"That is mandroid Constance, who is eight years old and don't ask me to explain it because it will take too much time." Thor studied the elaborate sand castle his daughter had constructed, knelt down beside her with Mary Bell and stated, "You have one great imagination to build something with so much detail with pathways, bridges, and the building's. What are these little things on the wall?"

"It is not my imagination Daddy. It is a military installation on the planet Kylee that is about 5 square miles with twenty-foot-high walls with energy cannons every thousand feet."

Thor held his computer watch over the sand construction and took a few pictures. He then heard his wife holler from the cottage. "Tippy! Get me a barf bucket! Abbie, I need clean bed sheets from the linen closet for Belinda's bed!"

Thor turned to Mary Bell and stated, "Get Chrissy and fast."

As the sprite took off, Cherry walked out of the cottage and paused on the front porch and reported, "Hon, Belinda is sick."

"I already sent Mrs. Bell for the Doc."

"Are you sure sending Mary Bell was a wise decision? You know how she manages to get into trouble without even trying."

"I know Mrs., Bell use to act before thinking. But she is a married woman now, with a level head on her shoulders. So, relax."

"I guess you are right. It's hard for me to picture Mary Bell that way after all the bruises, broken bones, scraps and cuts she had received these past years. Hey you must go. I'm sorry I won't be there to help you battle those huge black hairy spiders that drop down from the trees or those large, shaggy apes like creatures that want to use you as a snack."

"I know Kylee is not exactly a resort planet. Now, give me, a kiss so I can be on my way."

Later, as Thor was passing the Arboretum's pink rose trellis entrance, he saw one of the Institute's male staff holding a knife to Cathy Loganbury's throat threatening to kill her if anyone came near Star Fire Two. Thor touched his computer watch and said, "Lacy, patch me through to King Mex."

Three seconds later, the King answered and asked, "How can I help you?"

"I need your best archer at the entrance to the Arboretum. He needs to do a belly skin across the lake and tree dodge through the jungle, so he is not seen. When he gets here I will give him his instructions."

"He'll be there in five minutes, King Mex out."

Four minutes later, a three-foot-tall male sprite clad in green tapped Thor's leg and inquired, "What is it you want me to do?"

Thor pointed to the man in front of Star Fire Two's side hatch and stated, "I need you to place an arrow right between his eyes without harming the woman. Can you, do it?"

"Does the ground get wet when it rains?"

"Just do it."

The archer flew to a huge Shade Tree growing on the left side of the Botanical garden and waited for the right moment. Thor walked to the space craft and said, "Let Cathy go or die."

"Drop your energy pistol or I will slit her throat!"

Thor Whispered to Sam, "See if you can get his attention off Cathy." Thor drew his attention to Cathy and asked, "How are your legs holding up? I am surprised they haven't buckled on you by now."

Cathy let her knees buckle just as Sam caught the thug's attention causing him to look to his right. At that moment, a wooden arrow pierced his temple, Cathy dove for the tarmac as the man fell dead.

The sprite archer, landed next to Thor saluted him and reported, "Mission accomplished, Sir. Would you mind if I visit Mimi?"

"Sure, why don't you bring her a snack from the cafeteria? By the way what is your name?"

"Elmer, Sir."

"Here is an Institute pass that will permit you to see Mini any time you like."

"Thanks Sir!" and flew off."

Sam stared at the dead staff member and asked, "Is there a reason why you killed him?"

"He's not part of the Institute's staff and it was either kill him or have him kill Cathy.

Cathy gave Thor a hug saying, "Thanks Sir. For a while there I thought I was going to be talking to Jesus face to face."

"Take the rest of the day off."

Thor picked up Gideon, turned to Sam and Patrick and stated, "It's time we made tracks for Kylee."

Just then, Susie raced up to Thor as he was closing the side hatch and pleaded, "Sir oh please can you locate my husband Tom for me?"

"You two have a fight?"

"No, somebody shoved a picture of me in bed with another man under my front door this morning. Tom saw it and walked out on me."

"You shouldn't have been cheating your husband and you would not have been caught."

Susie showed Thor the photo of her and Rock in bed and said, "It's a lie!"

"When did, this romantic interlude supposed to take place?"

"Yesterday."

"Rock has been away for two days. Don't worry I'll have Tom back in your arms in on time."

CHAPTER 21

The Mad World

Forty-five minutes later, Thor landed Star Fire Two in the parking lot of a favorite watering hole called 'The Purple Goose,' on Avalon Prime. Sam stared at Thor and questioned, "This isn't Kylee?"

"Sorry, I've been preoccupied. It seems someone is circulating nude photos of the staff around the Institute. I got one and Susie received one yesterday and Tom walked out on her."

"Dora found one of me and Rose skinny dipping, tacked to our door the other day. Dora laughed and tore it up."

"When we get back I am going to put a stop to this shenanigan once and for all. Right now, Sam you are with me. Gideon and Patrick stay here and guard the ship."

Thor walked up to the bar in The Purple Goose placed his arm on Tom's back and said, "You do not have permission to leave the Institute and your wife didn't cheat on you. Some sick puppy is passing around fake photos of the male staff members."

The bartender put a drink in front of Tom saying, "Here is your Zombie."

Tom pushed Thor's arm off him and growled, "Get away from me!"

"You are going back to the Institute whether you like it or not." Thor showed the photo to Tom and asked, "Is this the picture?"

"Yeah That's Rock with my wife. What of it?"

"News flash. Rock was away on a mission. So, this can't be him."

"Then who is it?" roared Tom.

"No one. It is a composite picture."

Tom stared at the photo and remarked, "Hey you're right. My wife doesn't have a birthmark on her stomach."

Thor, Tom, and Sam turned around to leave and saw six men with broken bottles in their hands. Thor shook his head saying, "Gentlemen, you don't want to do this. Someone is bound to get hurt."

Sam took the metal baton from his belt, pressed the button, and extended it to a full javelin.

Thor leveled his energy pistil at the mob and said, "Back away or be sent to the hospital. The choice is yours."

One charged Thor with a knife in his hand. Thor fired a short blast sending him to the floor with a burned mark on his chest. The rest rushed forward, Sam held his javelin horizontally in front of him and shoved knocking everyone to the floor. Thor shot a light fixture and stated, "The next one to make a stupid move will be vaporized."

Back in Star Fire Two, Thor contacted the Institute and said, "Tell Susie her husband will be going with me to Kylee before returning home to her. Thor out."

Thor landed Star Fire Two on top of a large outcrop, handed out the energy rifles and said, "If it moves shoot it; before you become its next meal."

Tom inquired, "This planet can't be that bad Sir. Is it?"

Thor pointed skyward at a black bird with a dark blue head and a wingspan of eighteen feet soaring overhead and said, "Don't move, or you'll be its next meal."

Tom slowly raised his energy rifle and fired at the bird. Hitting it in its chest. The bird let out a loud screech and did a power dive for Tom. Thor shouted, "Head for the jungle it can't get us there!"

Sam yanked Tom's rifle out of his hand and hollered, "Don't just stand there, son get your butt in gear!"

In the safety of the tropical forest, Sam got in Tom's face and growled, "Of all the stupid, lamebrain, half-witted, idiotic things to do! What part of stand still, don't you understand? You never, never shoot at something that large and live to tell about it!"

"Sorry, Sir."

"There is a reason they call this the Mad Planet. Now, either follow instructions, or be ripped apart by something that defies description."

Thor handed Tom his rifle and stated, "We need to go to the Lost Valley and talk to O'Hara and see if he knows where this instillation that Constance told me about."

"Maybe we can leave Tom there." grumbled Sam.

"Let's go, the waterfalls isn't too far from here."

At the waterfalls, Thor pushed a large protruding rock in the cliff, stopping the water and draining the water in the pond at the base of the falls. Patrick picked up Gideon, and said, "I'll bring up the rear, just in case junior here decided to pull another boner."

At the bottom of the huge well, they turned left through a passageway into the Lost Valley some sixty miles long and twenty miles wide. Thor paused and gazed at the city that filled valley said, "We go right to the stone pillar and O'Hara's people are only a few miles from there."

Patrick tapped Thor's leg and said, "Don't you mean me people? And if we go your way it'll take us 2 days to get there. Follow me to the open-air tram and we'll be there in half an hour."

In the open tram, Tom leaned over and whispered, "Does everyone in this valley resemble leprechauns?"

"Yup. You are in 'The Valley of the Little of Kylee.'

Later, Patrick greeted the leader O'Hara and said, "Sir. I wish lodging for my friends. We are here to take out Woody P. Juarez. The one responsible for all the Blue Scarlet attacks around the Alliance."

"Ah yes. Him. Somehow, he reactivated the fail-safe system again. That's why you see all the weird things roaming around. Do me a favor, Thor. When you stomp on Woody, destroy the system so no one can use it again. Oh, his facility is on the other side of the planet. Don't worry I will show you a faster way to get there." O'Hara clapped his hands and 6 maidens clad in traditional Irish clothes pushed a table out on a white marble patio for Thor and his group to sit at. The Maidens placed a large cast iron pot of Irish stew, versions types of meat and seafood dishes on the table. O'Hara stated, "Dig in."

Thor inquired, "How long has Woody been on Kylee?"

"Oh, I'd say about 8 months of that I am aware of. But no more than 2 years."

"Then explain to me how he was able to build a fortress some 5 miles square?"

"He didn't. Some tall brown dude with short white hair and stubble on his back that looks like he once had wings. He wasn't sociable. When we found him 5 years ago, so we left him alone. Is there something about this guy I should know?"

Thor remain silent in disbelief. He then inquired, "By any chance does he happen to look like a will-o'-the-wisp?"

"My man didn't want to get that close to him because of the jagged makeshift sword he carries. But from the description my men have told me I'd would say, yes."

Thor muttered, "This mission just got serious."

Sam interjected, "It can't be Agar. General, our security lion made short work of whim 5 years ago."

"I'm not going to take any chances Sam."Thor turned to O'Hara and asked, "Can you do a recon mission for me? I need to see some photos of Agar and the surrounding area before we go in."

"I'll have my men get right on it."

An Irish maiden spotted Gideon and squealed, "Oh how cute! Is he your mascot?"

Patrick answered, "He is our Messenger Bear and one of the best fighters in the galaxy when it comes to handling the blade. Our computer expert designed him with a simple go and fetch program. But the program took on a life all its own and the end results is him. And yes, he loves to cuddle with people. Just make sure his katanas don't stab you."

The next morning, O'Hara set up a one-foot square cube on the marble table, touched one of the corner and a three-dimensional layout of the installation appeared. O'Hara stated, "This is the layout you requested."

Thor pointed to the north corner of the complex and inquired, "Can you zoom in on this area?"

"Sure can." O'Hara touched the three-dimensional image, intently enlarging that area. Thor stared at the rows and rows of solders standing in formation and stated, "There has to be at least five thousand men or more in that compound. This does not look good for our side."

"I can give you charge of my men which should even the odds."

"How are we going to defeat an army of men 6 feet tall with a bunch of leprechauns?"

"You would be surprised what we folk can do."

"What? Get stomped on." stated Sam.

O'Hara called some of his security guards and stated, "Let's show Thor what we can do. You ten men form a triangle. Patrick, throw that dish in the air."

The ten leprechauns quickly rubbed their hands together, grabbed the shoulders of the one in front of them as Patrick launched the plate. The point man clasped his hands and threw his arms up, sending a four inch in diameter charge of lightning out of his hands disintegrating the dish. O'Hara asked with a smile, "Any questions?"

Thor stared at O'Hara in unbelief and asked, "You mean all your people can expel lightning from their fingers?"

"Oh yeah. But it's something we try and keep a secret."

Understood. So, when do you suggest we get this invasion started?"

"You and your men set out for the fort and me and my men will meet you there."

"That fort is over seven thousand miles from here and will take us a good week to get there. I'd use Star Fire Two, but it will be picked up on their scanners before we even get close."

O'Hara handed Thor a 6-inch square computer board and instructed, "Plug this into your communication's computer. It will send out a jamming signal and make your craft invisible to all scanning devices. When you get within ten miles of the fort, drop down to treetop level and land in the field. Then hike in from there."

"Thanks. Where do you want to meet?"

"I will find you. Good luck and good hunting my friend."

In Star Fire Two, Patrick inserted the computer board and stated, "All set Boss."

Thirty-four minutes later Thor landed the spacecraft in a huge green meadow, contacted the Institute, and said, "Rock, I need you to give a message to my daughter, Abbie."

"Sure, thing Sir."

"Give her my coordinates and tell her that I need her assistance A-S-A-P."

A minute later, Abbie rushed in the side hatch and clad in a green slack suit, inquired, "What's up Dad?"

In the ship's lounge, Thor showed his daughter a photo of Woody and Agar. Gave her a camera and instructed, "Change into some camouflage clothes, then I want you to fly west and scout out the military base. I want to see if Agar is the one behind these brutal Blue Scarlet attacks."

"Be back in a flash Dad."

Patrick inquired, "What would you guys like to eat? Grinder, hoagie, torpedo, hero, or a sub?"

"How about a nice pot of Coconut-hazelnut coffee." stated Thor.

"I have that too.

Tom inquired, "What about asking Prince Blue for help? The last time I heard he was itching for some payback after those attacks on Willow City. Especially if Agar is involved."

"He'd be good for backup in case O'Hara's men fail." stated Sam.

"Food first than I'll call Blue."

Thirty minutes later, Abbie stormed in the side hatch with several burn marks on her back and grumbled, "The idea of that guy coming on to me like that, I sure fixed his wagon."

Thor stared at his daughter and said, "I take it you were spotted."

"A soldier came up behind me and grabbed my butt when I was trying to sneak up to the base."

"I take it you taught him how to sing soprano."

"Nope, I taught him how to fly. Boy, did he ever go splat. I don't think it was Woody."

"Grab yourself a grinder, and a cup of coffee than we'll look at the photos."

Later, Abbie showed her father the pictures she took and stated, "Dad. We defiantly have a problem. Agar is in command of the five-thousand weird men. They are plant reproductions, but Agar has found a way to give life to them."

"Meaning?"

"If you cut off an arm, a new one quickly grows back. Plain arrows and energy weapons will not stop them. The only way to defeat Agar's army is to kill all of them, all at once. If we don't, the Alliance is will be no more."

Sam spoke up and said, "What if we defeat Agar, his plant army might go in a state of confusion."

"Agar also has about a thousand real men ready to take over in case something goes wrong."

Tom entered the conversation and stated, "Sir. The lab has found out the plant reproductions are highly flammable. If we can ignite the plant army while they are in formation. It will be like dropping a match in a field of dry grass."

O'Hara knocked on the side hatch door of Star Fire Two, Patrick opened it and said, "Come on in Sir."

Thor explained, "Have your men set up in the upper left corner of the compound then shoot the plant solders with flaming arrows. That should take care of Agar's army. Sam, Tom, Gideon, and I will sneak in and take out the ammo dump.

O'Hara smiled and said, "You guys wanna come outside for a moment?"

Everyone stepped out of the spacecraft and saw the field crowded with huge black bird with a dark blue head this is my air force."

"I thought those birds were part of this Mad Planet," stated Thor.

"They are. But we found a way to train them. Of course, some Dingbat wounded one of my birds the other day leaving me a man short. So, what is your game plan?"

"You create a diversion, by attacking the men on the base, Sam, Tom, Gideon, Patrick and I will go after Woody and Agar."

"What about me Dad?" Asked Abbie.

"You stay in the ship. I don't want you getting hurt."

"Ah, Dad. Are you forgetting that I am a Will-o`-the-wisp and can take anything those Creeps can throw at me?"

O'Hara had his birds carry some of his Thor's group three miles from Agar's fort and stated, "When my men attack, go for it."

A half mile from Agar's defensive structure, Thor signaled everybody to hide because of a passing patrol. Abbie whispered, "Dad. Wait here. I can take care of those Losers."

Abbie casually walked up to the detachment with a forlorn expression on her face and said, "Excuse me fells but I seem to be a bit lost."

"This is a military instillation ma'am and you're gonna have to come with us."

"Oh, a Sir. What about my friends? Do you want them to come along too?"

Thor and the others sprang up from behind several bushes with their energy rifles pointed at them. Abbie smiled and stated, "Did I tell you that I am part of an attack party. Kindly drop your weapons."

The commander growled, "You're out numbered, so it's your men who have to surrender."

Patrick stepped forward, quickly rubbed his hands together and stretched them out in front of him sending several bolts of electricity from his fingers, immobilizing the commander and his men.

CHAPTER 22

Agar's Last Stand

At the huge fortress, Thor and his men hunkered down and waited for O'Hara's signal. Minutes later, a huge flock of birds flew overhead triggering an alarm. Four men quickly emerged from their hiding places brandishing high powered energy rifles. Sam whispered, "They don't look like plant men. Shall we send Gidester to take care of them?"

Gideon Bear slowly waddled up to the men, handed them a note that read, give up, or die."

The man stared at the bear, laughed, and said, "This has to be a joke. Waste the thing!"

Gideon reached behind him, took his katanas in his paws, and leaped in the air, slicing off one man's head. The other three quickly fired at the bear but killed each other in the confusion.

Thor stared up at the impenetrable fortress and asked, "Sam, Tom, any ideas how we are going to get in?"

A tall blue Will-o`-the-wisp clad in golden regal armor tapped Thor's shoulder and said, "Allow my men to make a hole for you."

"Prince Blue. Where did you come from?"

"Your daughter Tippy told me that Agar might be the one who caused all the trouble in the galaxy. So, here I am." Prince Blue turned and let go a loud Will-o`-the-wisp war cry that triggered eight thousand turquoise Wisp to respond with a low roar sending out a shock wave that pulverized a huge section of the wall. Prince Blue then said to Thor, "After you."

Inside the fortress, Blue bellowed, "Agar! Your time has come to die!"

A few hundred plant men charged Blue's men with Woody in the lead. Agar stepped into view, and commanded his men to halt, glared at Prince Blue, and stated through clenched teeth, "You can't stop me Blue and you know it. I'll be back with a much stronger army."

"Look behind you, Agar. You have nowhere to go."

The disgraced Will-o`-the-wisp glanced over his left shoulder and saw O'Hara's birds had formed a line behind his men. Blue let go a bloodcurdling screech, signaling eight thousand turquoise Will-o-the-wisp to attack. Before Agar's men had a chance to fire a single shot, screams rang out. When the last of Agar's army fell, he was marched up to Prince Blue. Agar glared at Blue and smirked, "You are not going to kill me, and you know it."

The Prince slowly removed his jewel encrusted sword from its sheath, rested the point on Agar's chest and stated, "You are a disgrace to the Will-o'-the-wisp race with all the carnage you've caused." Blue lowered his sword, to his side and stated, "Thousands of humans are crying out from their graves to be avenge, and they shall have it!" in one smooth stroke from Blue's sword and Agar's head was severed from his body. The Prince stared at the lifeless body of Agar, then drove his sword through his heart, to make sure he was dead.

Woody approached Thor with his hands up saying, "Looks like I will be going back with you to the Institute where all those beautiful women are."

"Not this time Woody. Your fate awaits you."

Woody glanced up and saw a black bird with a dark blue head standing behind him. He smiled sheepishly and said, "I guess that's my ride back."

Thor nodded, the bird picked Woody up by his head, tossed him in the air, caught him swallowing him whole.

Blue turned to his men and stated, "Repair the fortress, this looks like a good place to setup an outpost. If it is alright with you, O'Hara."

"Does this mean this planet will no longer be known as the Mad World?"

"Yes."

"Great, as long as your men, clean up all the dead bodies."

Epilogue

Back on the hidden planetoid where the Institute is. Thor collapsed on the front porch of his cottage, Constance jumped in his lap and gave him a welcome home hug and asked, "Can I play dress up with Gideon? Can I Daddy? Can I? Can I?"

"If it is alright with Gidester, you can."

Gideon Bear stared at Thor as if to say, "I'm gonna get you for this as Constance picked him up to put a dress on him.

Cherry handed Thor a cup of Coconut-Hazelnut coffee and said, "We have guest for the evening meal. So, hurry up and get ready. Oh, Tom and Susie made up."

Thor set up a table on the sand fifty feet from the cottage, placed some tike torches around it, then helped Cherry set the table. Mary Bell approached with Jay carrying their baby Alisha he handed the baby to Mary Bell and took a fighting stance when he saw Todd walking towards them clad in a white tuxedo. Thor immediately stepped in and said, "Back off Jay, Todd is our guest this evening." Thor turned to Todd and asked, "Is there something you wanted to say to Mrs. Bright?"

Mary Bell swallowed heard, gave Alisha, to Cherry, put on a pleasant smile and said, "It's so nice to see you Todd. I never knew you owned a tux."

Todd, lowered his head and stated, "We've been buds for years, and I don't blame you if you don't forgive me. But, I have to say my piece. I am sorry for doing all those awful things to you. Can you find it in your heart to forgive me?"

Mary Bell stared at Todd in silence, Todd slowly turned to walk away, Mary Bell, caught him by his right arm, gave him a hug saying, "Welcome back."

www.ingramcontent.com/pod-product-compliance
Lightning Source LLC
Chambersburg PA
CBHW020521120726
47904CB00003B/918

* 9 7 8 1 6 4 4 6 0 0 6 3 4 *